PITY THE GENIUS

A JOURNEY THROUGH AMERICAN GUITAR MUSIC IN 33 TRACKS

JOEL HARRISON

CYMBAL PRESS

Pity the Genius: A Journey through American Guitar Music in 33 Tracks
© 2024 Joel Harrison. All rights reserved.

Published by Cymbal Press, Torrance, CA USA
cymbalpress.com

This and other Cymbal Press books may be purchased at cymbalpress.com. Volume and education discounts are available.

ISBN
Paperback: 978-1-955604-16-1
Hardcover: 978-1-955604-17-8

MUS023060	MUSIC / Musical Instruments / Guitar
MUS055000	MUSIC / Essays
MUS050000	MUSIC / Individual Composer & Musician
BIO004000	BIOGRAPHY & AUTOBIOGRAPHY / Music

All marks are the property of their respective owners.

Publisher: Gary S. Stager
Editor: Sylvia Martinez
Cover: Yvonne Martinez

While every precaution has been taken, the publisher and author assume no responsibility for errors, omissions, changed information or URLs, or for damages resulting from the use of the information herein.

Advance Praise for
Pity the Genius: A Journey through American Guitar Music in 33 Tracks

"This is really profound, evocative stuff—Joel is not only a great player, he's a great writer. Everyone should read this book."
—Mike Stern: Jazz Guitarist

"*Pity the Genius* reads like a memoir told through the lens of a listener, student and friend of pivotal, emotionally complex, guitar innovators of the 20th century. Joel Harrison takes the reader on a deeply personal tour that highlights the musical contributions and the humanity behind the artists."
— Randy Napoleon: Associate Professor of Jazz Guitar & Associate Director of Jazz Studies, Michigan State University

"What a wonderful series of essays. While Harrison is writing about guitarists, his subject really is how people deal with the need to make art, what happens at the intersection of creativity and personality. And Harrison was there: Allan Holdsworth, Danny Gatton, you're finding out what it was like to be in their presence, what the world was like then, what was expected, what happened. Deep, deep stuff, sometimes profoundly sad, sometime ecstatic, but always illuminating."
— Peter Watrous: *NY Times* jazz critic 1986-2000

"Music is one of the most glorious professions, but it's also among the cruelest. For every original artist who makes it over, there are hundreds who remain confined to the shadows, forever exiled from mainstream—or any—recognition. In *Pity the Genius*, a collection of tributes to maverick guitarists many of whom never got their due while they were alive, Joel Harrison rescues his subjects from what E.P. Thompson called "the enormous condescension of posterity." He captures the music they left behind in a deeply American prose, full of wit and existential wisdom, and refreshingly free of the pretentious cant often disguised as 'music criticism.'"
— Adam Schatz: US editor *The London Review of Books*, contributor to *NY Times Review of Books*

"Joel Harrison has created a book that every serious guitar player should, and will no doubt want to, read. It's as comprehensive a collection of profiles as I've ever seen. He's presented us with an eclectic but seriously comprehensive list of players from Snoozer Quinn to Pat Martino to Jimmy Wyble, Thumbs Carlisle, Danny Gatton, Dennis Budimir and many more extraordinary and smart choices. I can't think of a good guitarist who wouldn't think of this book as a delightful way to spend an evening and learn about this amazing art form."
— Jim Carlton: regular contributor to *Vintage Guitar Magazine*; columnist for *Just Jazz Guitar Magazine*. Author of *Conversations With Great Jazz and Studio Guitarists* - Mel Bay Publishing

"It is rare to find an accomplished musician who is also an accomplished, insightful writer. Joel Harrison's *Pity the Genius* is the best of both worlds. Harrison finds the brightest light and the most secret dark in his subjects, and writes them out so they become, for a while, your own experience. If you are at all curious about the phenomenon of obscure mastery, including perhaps your own, read this book. *Pity the Genius* is a clear source of self-awareness for writer and reader alike."
— W.A. Mathieu: Composer/ educator/ Author of *The Listening Book*

Table of Contents

Introduction	1
Arthur Rhames Live at My Father's Place	7
Pat Martino You Don't Know What Love Is	13
Danny Gatton Harlem Nocturne	17
Roscoe Holcomb Boat's Up the River	25
Emily Remler Ode to Mali	29
Allan Holdsworth Sphere of Innocence	35
Blind Willie Johnson God Moves On The Water	43
Mick Goodrick Vox Humana	45
Jimi Hendrix Machine Gun	49
Jimmy Wyble Roly Poly	53
Roy Buchanan Sweet Dreams	57
Snoozer Quinn Lover Come Back to Me / On the Alamo	63
Sister Rosetta Tharpe Guitar Solos	67
David Lindley Call It a Loan	71
"Thumbs" Carllile Springfield Social Club	75
Prince *with Vernon Reid* The Ride	79

Jerry Garcia   87
    Dark Star

John Abercrombie   93
    Ghost Dance

Sonic Youth *by Nels Cline*   97
    Brave Men Run (In My Family)

Ritchie Blackmore   103
    Speed King

Ralph Towner   107
    Nimbus

Cornell Dupree *by Adam Levy*   111
    Bridge Over Troubled Water—Aretha Franklin

Joni Mitchell and Larry Carlton   115
    Amelia

Willie King   119
    I Am the Blues

Jim Hall   125
    Scrapple From the Apple

Hubert Sumlin *by Elliott Sharp*   131
    Goin' Down Slow

Lenny Breau with Chet Atkins   137
    Polka Dots and Moonbeams

Kurt Rosenwinkel   141
    Ezra

Elliot Ingber *by Henry Kaiser*   145
    Alice in Blunderland

Vic Juris   149
    Time Remembered

Derek Trucks   153
    Gravity

Dennis Budimir *with Bill Frisell*   157
    The Blues, Sprung Free

Curtis Mayfield   163
    People Get Ready

Afterword   167
About the Authors   171
Photo Credits   173
Also from Cymbal Press   175

Introduction

A childhood memory returned to me as I was finishing this book. All the wild men and women and their astonishing stories dredged it up—their exultation, their sorrows, the ripple effect of their genius.

My uncle John, whom I barely knew, was an astonishingly good jazz pianist. In the rare times he travelled from Manhattan to visit my family in Washington D.C. he would spend most of the day at the zoo, apparently preferring the company of animals to humans. He had eyes that never settled on anything, he wouldn't look at you when he talked. Even as a kid I could sense the furtive loneliness in them. John mostly dressed in brown, perfectly shined oxfords, a rumpled dress white shirt, a thin, stained tie, and tweed pants that looked two sizes too small. He wore a trench coat that he was reticent to remove and sported a beige fedora on a balding head. Sometimes he would cringe if engaged in conversation, turn his face away, and hold up his trembling palm as if to ward off all human contact. In hindsight I suspect he was autistic. He would spend days in Union Station feeding the pigeons or sitting in hotel lobbies. Detectives from the hotels would eventually evict him. He fascinated and scared me.

Later in life I came to understand that his childhood wasn't easy—his parents' character and disposition could have frozen boiling water, and I'm guessing he grew up feeling very alone. But one thing they *did* grant him was piano lessons. He had talent and a promising future, but he was too dysfunctional to make a career of music. I doubt he ever played live. Mary, his Chinese wife, was also a pianist. She'd been born into privilege in Shanghai, attended the conservatory at an early age, and was molded to be a great concert soloist. She'd won competitions and was set to go study in New York at one of the best schools. But the revolution came, her parents were suddenly impoverished, and her education ended. Like Uncle John she kept playing, but never for others.

I recall hearing them only once. This must have been 1965, I was eight years old. John and Mary arrived for a holiday visit and my parents begged them to play our gleaming baby grand piano. They both said no. Aunt Mary said she wasn't good enough, and John merely shrugged and stayed glued to his chair. Somehow, though, the coaxing paid off. What happened next changed my life.

Mary was first—she carefully settled her thin, frail body on the piano bench, adjusted the height, and for a moment there was a suspenseful silence as she rubbed her palms together. Then she lifted her hands high and hurled them onto the keys. There was an eruption of sound that to my young ears was as shocking as a bomb going off. This was no plaintive waltz. It was a virtuosic blast of arpeggios from the bottom to the top of the instrument, Liszt perhaps, or Beethoven, fortissimo, fast, dramatic, and impassioned. The whole family was bug-eyed. I felt as if my head popped off my body. But she made one mistake, and within 90 seconds she abruptly stopped. In her broken English she said emphatically, "I no good enough now." We pleaded with her to continue, but she refused. I was terribly disappointed. How on earth could someone this good believe otherwise?

Now it was John's turn. Dad requested some Gershwin. John shambled over to the piano looking as if he was being punished, and the second bomb exploded. He launched into an upbeat tune in what I would later learn was the florid, swinging style of Teddy Wilson. His left hand charged through the changes in blasts of bass as he added thick chords and a right-hand melody. His hands would cross over, voices moving every which way. Like Mary he had extraordinary technique, a type of

Uncle John

finesse and style that I'd never dreamed of. The piano seemed to lift from the ground in celebration. It was used to "Chopsticks," it had never been treated to such excellence. Here was this total oddball, a stranger to language, custom, and convention producing the sounds of the gods in my living room. How could such happy, buoyant music come from such a troubled man? A miracle had occurred. When he was done, I knew what I wanted to do with my life.

I never saw my uncle again. Two years later I awoke at 4am to hear my mother pleading into the telephone, "Mary, please calm yourself … Mary, tell me what happened." I could hear the sound of hysterical wailing from the other end of the phone as I stood wide-eyed in my pajamas. Uncle John had been murdered outside a jazz club in Harlem, shot in the back of the head. The motive was a mystery, the killer was never found, and I doubt anyone tried terribly hard to find any answers.

Years later I visited the tiny rent-regulated apartment Mary and John had lived in. She was in her 80s and still there. The curtains were drawn. No light entered from the street. Two Steinway baby grand pianos sat facing each other in one of the two rooms. They took up so much space that there was barely room for a couch. I gently pressed a few keys. The gorgeous instruments were coated in a thin layer of grime and dust and terribly out of tune. I figured neither had been touched since John died 35 years back, now monuments to silence. The melancholy of what might have been hung like a veil about the room.

Many beloved musicians were, like my uncle, immune to convention, or anything resembling "normal behavior." More than a few suffered, struggled, some acutely, and clearly used music not just to get by, but to survive. I've found there are only three antidotes to the insanity of the world we live in—the love of another human being, the untamed wilds of nature, and art. In this book I honor a few of those who with a guitar managed to bring some shape, beauty, and love into our lives. I chose them first for their mastery, but also because they lived in shadows, and they merit the attention we never afforded them when they were here. In some tiny way my uncle John was part of this family. His whole life was one big shadow. He was a ghost in this world, friendless save for his wife, a man who lived so far on the fringe of the known world that he barely existed at all.

But I know he performed once. It was a small audience in a living room in Washington D.C. that included an eight-year-old boy whose eyes and ears, once opened, could never again close.

Mastering an instrument can be a liability. Amongst guitar players, Charlie Christian was dead by 25, Eddie Lang by 30, Hendrix and Robert Johnson by 27. Danny Gatton and Roy Buchanan both killed themselves. Snoozer Quinn stopped playing in his 30s and disappeared, mostly because of booze, only to be found in a tuberculosis sanitarium and finally recorded weeks away from death at age 42.

Mastery comes at a cost. Many begin the journey, few go all the way. Going all the way means you put in the time. You give yourself over to the instrument. It's a state of mind, maybe a mania that you're born with. It's a never-ending discovery, one that's full of high excitement and miserable drudgery. Each of the artists in this collection have gone all the way. They staked out a vision and fought for it. Quite a few were mentors who never made it into the magazines and newspapers. When I've written about a well-known player, I've done so because I felt I had a personal and perhaps unusual perspective.

The title of the book, *Pity the Genius*, began as a placeholder. Then it began to speak to me. Three quarters of the way through I realized that a good number of my subjects had lives no one in their right mind would choose. Sometimes it seemed that the more gifted, the higher the price—depression, addiction, disease. And yet! Those players brought joy to numberless listeners, even when they were not able to experience that joy themselves.

But this book is not about tragedy. Romanticizing artists' hardships, as Clint Eastwood did in the movie *Bird*, is not my goal. My aim is celebration and gratitude. It's the music that lives on, not the madness. I hope my passion for what these artists have given us inspires more research and curiosity, because the instrument tells a story of America you won't find in a history book or on social media. The guitar is funky, noisy, sweet, intimate, and horribly outrageous. It makes people sing, dance, tear their clothes off on a mud-drenched field surrounded by acidhead lunatics. It's been a weapon in the march for peace and a

Introduction

cudgel in the style of music called Death Metal. Guitarists cause dictators to summon the police. Its holy stages are juke joints, back-alley bars, enormous, hippie-drenched festivals— not so much Carnegie Hall.

Hoping for as much objectivity as possible I decided to ask some esteemed colleagues to offer up their own essays. More voices add depth to the collection, and I've always been a collaborator. I made a conscious decision, with a couple of exceptions, not to write about friends and people whom I interviewed in my previous book *Guitar Talk*. That wasn't easy. Some of the guitarists I respect the most are contemporaries and colleagues.

Finally, if you think you're about to read something akin to "Rolling Stone's Top 100 Guitar Players," return the book now. This collection is a snapshot taken with love, no more. Countless masters, including some who have been most formative for me, were left out. The artists in this book are part of a great story still being told. Perhaps you may discover a player you'd never known. Just as importantly, though, this book may encourage you to turn back to an artist you already are passionate about and perceive an even deeper value in their gift.

Gratitude Department

Henry Kaiser for always having an answer to some obscure guitar inquiry.

My guest contributors for their time and passion.

Jeff Siegel, John Esposito, Vernon Reid, Matt Munisteri, Chulo Gatewood, Russell Malone, John Previti, Larry Koonse, Dave Liebman, Gil Goldstein, Pete Van Allen, and Jim Carlton for valuable insights into my subjects.

"A genius is a person most like himself."
—*Thelonious Monk*

Arthur Rhames

Live at My Father's Place

(1978)

There is virtually no record of Arthur's life on earth save scratchy recordings from basements or parks, out-of-print blowing sessions on vinyl, a couple of grainy YouTube videos, and the testimony of friends, now in their 60s and 70s, still stunned and searching for superlatives to describe someone no one really knew.

Arthur grew up in the Brownsville section of Brooklyn in the 1960s. He had a difficult upbringing and left home at age sixteen, living for a time at the Hare Krishna temple in downtown Brooklyn. Arthur styled himself as a blues rock guitar player in the mode of Johnny Winter, and by high school he was besting all the local competition. In the battle of bands at Brooklyn Tech Arthur always won, and in an incredibly short period of time, around 1972, he expanded exponentially upon his blues-rock foundation and began playing torrents of notes as if Robert Johnson, Coltrane, McLaughlin, and Hendrix had all found a common body.

The recordings we have of of his guitar playing are shadows, suggestions, which is why I've chosen a YouTube clip to represent him playing with his volcanic trio, Eternity. (youtu.be/lKfqhHZprws) Everyone who heard him live said you had to see it to believe it, incredible dexterity, a new guitar vocabulary built at that burgeoning nexus of modern jazz and rock.

He formed Eternity in the mid-1970s with Cleveland Alleyne on bass and Collin Young on drums. The music from this concert video sounds like a sort of exorcism, howls and wails like someone running from a burning building. His tone is searing, distorted, blues-drenched. The high-speed melodies and wide leaps are virtuosic—fast, and incredibly precise rhythmically, clearly the result of obsessive practicing.

You hear a deep stew of African American musical history in Arthur's sound. Obviously, he knew Hendrix intimately, you hear his R&B roots, and then the extrapolation and fragmenting of those roots into the free jazz of the moment. Legend has it that he'd play a virtuoso lick and then do the same thing with his left hand draped over the neck. Arthur hardly slept, he would sometimes practice eighteen hours a day, often in the park. He was always broke, he couch-surfed, and was both winningly friendly and deeply private. Rhames often busked in Manhattan, and players such as Bill Frisell and Joe Lovano reported hearing him back in those times, out in Union Square, or around New York City. He was a closeted gay man and died of AIDS in 1989 at the age of 32.

The story becomes ever more impossible to absorb. Being a phenomenally gifted guitarist was insufficient. Rhames' first instrument was actually the tenor saxophone which he began when he was nine. He began playing guitar when he was fourteen. Then, incredibly, he mastered the piano.

Arthur Rhames in Prospect Park

Drummer Jeff Siegel, who was in Arthur's band in the early '80s, describes walking into his first gig with Arthur and seeing him on the keys sounding like a mix of Art Tatum and McCoy Tyner. Minutes later he learned Arthur was actually the sax player on the date. Only *later* did he learn Arthur's main instrument was guitar. I suppose it's redundant to point out that virtuosity on one instrument is rare, on two rather shocking. Three? Unheard of. If you've practiced for a 6- or 8-hour stretch you know it's grueling, the pleasure quotient wanes, and it becomes more about obsession, maybe desperation. Your bones ache, your brain starts to boil. 18 hours? How did he do it?

He was a man of huge appetites. At a diner after a gig he might consume two lamb sandwiches, two plates of pancakes, and multiple deserts. In his late twenties he began to obsessively lift weights. If you roomed with him after a gig you might not sleep, because all night long Rhames played guitar, sang Hare Krishna songs, listened to the cassette recording of the performance, and built his body. Arthur would spend the wee hours working out series of intervallic sequences that ate up the entire neck, licks that were very difficult to play. He sought a new language. His approach on the guitar differed from his approach on piano and saxophone. He believed each instrument had its own identity and should be dealt with in its own specific way. He was expert at standard jazz harmony on sax, for instance, but usually chose not to play that repertoire on guitar.

In the '80s Arthur played small clubs around New York City, wearing out everyone in his bands with burning tempos and marathon sets. He made a small income from playing in a popular R&B band at the time called Slave, but after a couple of years he quit the group. Arthur mostly didn't own his instruments; he would borrow guitars or horns, some of which seemed strung together by rubber bands. A Japanese video crew filmed him at the Jazz Forum, one of the only times he was professionally documented. The master tape was destroyed in a flood in the studio it was housed in before anyone could see it. No other copies survive. He toured as an opening act for Larry Coryell. The relationship was said to be fractious, Coryell dismissive of Rhames, Rhames demanding more recognition. Coryell banished him.

John Coltrane's bassist, Reggie Workman, called him a messenger.

Arthur, like other savants before him, had little idea how to live on planet earth. He slept in the park, got attacked and beat up, he wandered the streets, and for a time worked as a security guard in a peep show on 42nd Street. He recorded, but none of the records gained any purchase. The reasons seem to be made of fairy dust and voodoo curses. Apparently the only substantial press he got in years of gigging was a take-down in the *Village Voice* by the infamous critic Stanley Crouch. Crouch came to a set in the mid-1980s at Mikell's on the Upper West Side. Arthur would say of that gig that everyone was going wild except Crouch, who sat frowning with his arms crossed at a front table.

Recall Crouch was a gatekeeper for the so-called young lions in those days, a club Arthur would have had no interest in joining. Perhaps this was an avant-garde set that wasn't to Crouch's liking. But why would Crouch, who was one of the most intelligent, capable writers I ever met, take a cruel tone, savaging Rhames, making fun of not just his playing but how he dressed and looked? Crouch called him a Coltrane clone. If that was the case why would Coltrane's own bandmates, Elvin Jones, Rashied Ali, Reggie Workman, and even Coltrane's wife, Alice, get on stage with him? Clearly these figureheads thought he was dedicated to and capable of moving Coltrane's legacy forward. This type of personal attack from a jazz critic is, to me, disgusting and shameful, especially given Rhames' monstrous talent and dedication to his craft.

The Crouch article deeply depressed Arthur, and he pulled back from playing publicly. With no permanent place of residence, he lived for a while with a woman, who was also his manager and who was reputed to be a "hit-person" for the mafia. Arthur owed her money which he couldn't pay. She wanted to sleep with him which was a no-go, so she threatened to have him killed if he ever played in New York again. Rhames went into hiding upstate, living for a time with pianist John Esposito, who had been a frequent member of Arthur's group. While living there Arthur worked as a counselor for teens, largely set aside music and got into health foods and yoga.

Throughout his life Arthur hid his homosexuality, terrified of being rejected if any of his contemporaries knew. It's important to remember that at the time, even amongst the typically liberal jazz community, homophobia was rampant. As AIDS began to devour young men, people became not just prejudiced, but terrified of the gay community. I've been told by African American friends that in that time the Black church considered being gay a greater sin than being a thief or murderer. Vernon Reid, who considers Arthur a seminal influence, told me that Arthur was "afraid that if he was 'out' that all of us who loved and worshipped him as an artist would turn our backs on him." Vernon went on to say that his experience of accepting Arthur's homosexuality changed his views on the subject, and taught him the type of tolerance that is now more mainstream. I've heard other musicians say the same thing.

Vernon visited Arthur in the hospital at the end of his life and brought him a guitar. Ravaged by AIDS, Arthur played a few licks and said, with complete optimism, "When I get better and get out of here, I'm going to concentrate on the blues because this experience has given me a new insight into human suffering." The day before he was set to leave the hospital to recuperate at the home of a friend, he died.

Of Arthur's death John Esposito said in an extended conversation we had: "Someday there will be a reckoning and admission in human terms for how destructive our society's homophobia has been. This country has a terrible history of discarding human lives. How many Arthur Rhames-type scientists, writers, artists, inventors have been destroyed? Unfortunately, the male jazz community has been complicit in all this." After attending Rhames funeral, the great saxophonist John Stubblefield told Esposito that amongst his peers Rhames was talked about as the inheritor of the jazz legacy that extended from Armstrong through Charlie Parker and John Coltrane. You don't get that type of acclaim if you're an "imitator" or a "clone."

This brief flame of a life demands an explanation. But what is it? There's always a disconnect between what the culture values and what a visionary offers. But this chasm of a disconnect is something of a record-breaker. Pity the genius. Rhames staked out the impossible on his instrument. What are any of us willing to do, to sacrifice, to endure for what we believe in? He bent the guitar to his will. There was nothing safe about his choices. He was seeking freedom in the way Sun Ra did, and that freedom was a pinhole at the time, not a big, wide doorway. There's no doubt he would have had more recognition had he been white and straight. His struggle and demise were inextricably tied to the racist, homophobic, classist, and conformist culture of his era. And yet—Arthur remained committed to a goal of transcendence. He remained positive, he modelled devotion in the music community, doggedly rehearsing, studying, growing, workshopping, playing anywhere and everywhere. It was a spiritual journey for him.

Vernon Reid said to me that if Arthur Rhames could die broke and obscure, it suggests that the world is random, meaningless, and absent of justice. Music is not a meritocracy. We're left chewing on ambiguous concepts such as karma, luck, timing. It certainly didn't help his financial prospects to situate himself in the avant-garde. With all this ability couldn't Arthur have become a sideman to one of the reigning bandleaders? It's said that he could be tough to work with, tardy to gigs. This certainly affected potential employers. Also consider that he might blow away anyone else on the bandstand, and thus become something of a liability to a certain type of leader.

We have to see the positive. Arthur speaks to the infinite potential of the human race. A genius can emerge from anywhere, at any time, and inspire us all to give more, to be more, to sacrifice more. But the accompanying message is that the visionary, the emissary, is often a target. His or her heart, seemingly so strong, is easily cut in two.

More and more everyone sounds the same. Thank the internet. The obscurity of Arthur Rhames, and maybe the arc of such a life itself cannot happen again, because everyone copies the copiers now. YouTube has changed everything, made everyone a star in their own living room. Virtuosos are everywhere, but what is *not* everywhere are the dark, sharp, original edges that gave Arthur his sound, the lacerating energy that all but slaps you in the face. There was nothing pretty about this man's life or times. Those edges you can only develop in isolation, unobserved, where no one hears or understands you.

His ecstasy we gladly draw inspiration from. His anguish we can only surmise, and to do so we risk sentimentality. You could call him courageous. But people like Arthur don't have a choice, they're not thinking so much about a reward, they're just trying to unload the weight from their chests. Had he survived, he might have eventually broken through. Times have changed since 1980. But then, to play with that level of ferocity, to be that raw and rough, and be Black, and be gay? Any one of those things alone could have killed him.

Pat Martino

You Don't Know What Love Is

We'll Be Together Again (Muse Records 1976)

One of the benefits of getting older is that you start to see the layers of nuance and complexity behind what previously seemed simple. You begin to see that sometimes the best route really is the straightest line between two points. Youth tends to be discursive, unsettled, broiling with subplots. You get older and maybe you just want a player to reveal his heart, damn the hot licks. You delight in a ballad.

And so, I choose this track of Pat Martino's, which on the surface goes against reason. Isn't the essential thing about Pat his speed, his monster bebop dexterity? Defiantly, I say no. Everyone loves that aspect of his guitar playing, the hair-raising 16th notes on, say, "Impressions." But this track reveals his mastery of interpreting a melody.

This is a great jazz tune taken at a glacial tempo—the absence of a rhythm section, and the boldly spare pianism of Gil Goldstein allows for delicious space. The track feels weightless. Pat's phrases remind me of how Brando delivered some of his best lines in The Godfather. Brando has a furnace stoked inside yet only reveals a small glimpse of the heat. There's a dangerous intimacy you feel, he draws you in, yet holds more back. The timing—it's everything. Sometimes Pat (and Brando) wait a couple of beats to deliver a phrase, or maybe speeds into it only to quickly withdraw. It's heavy and light at the same time, vulnerable, but making no confessions.

The precision of Pat's execution is always devastating. The focus, the attack of his right hand, is positively Napoleonic. It's never inhuman, though, and in this piece it's like a lightning strike, a small explosion of light in the middle of charged air. His fills, in which he triples times the feel, are harmonically rich with bebop language, and they threaten to take over, but then he pulls in and we're back to that deep silence. Sorrow, perhaps. You truly hear the lyric when he plays:

You don't know what love is
'til you know the meaning of the blues
Until you've loved a love
You had to lose…

Without a doubt Pat knew the meaning.

I started by writing about age versus youth. Pat was only 35 years old when he made this record. But Pat was born old. How else to explain his blinding technique at age 14? He had most of what he needed before he went to his prom. I met him in 1975 when he was 31 years old and I interviewed him for my college radio show. Something about his presence made him seem like an elder sage. I don't know or care much about his life outside of music, which may well have been full of immaturity. I'm talking about the way he spoke, the stillness inside the inferno, the emphasis on spirit and finding truth in sound. His voice was very deep, odd because he was thin and small of stature, and that's what I hear in this track—a deep voice. Not long after this track was recorded he would have the aneurysm that would rob him of his memory and the ability to play guitar. In this time period he was beginning to have seizures, growing aware of the invisible enemy hiding in his brain.

Pat spent years reconstructing his memories and his ability to play the guitar. After a long period of recovery he had an entire second career, eventually sounding every bit as good as the "first Pat Martino." In a lesson I had with Pat in the mid-1990s he said something intriguing about this process. I asked him how he'd managed to find the strength and willpower to essentially start again from scratch. A few years before our lesson, I'd suffered from tendonitis of the wrist and had to stop playing for a while. So, my question to him was not rhetorical—there was a measure of desperation to it. How to love the instrument again when playing it felt so hard, when pain and creativity seemed to be bedfellows? Pat said his motivation was "boredom." Boredom? This seemed a rather mundane explanation—and then, upon reflection, quite deep. He seemed reluctant to extrapolate.

Pat Martino (2011)

He inferred that inactivity was destroying him. Pat was quite cryptic. What I took away was the feeling of being with him in the room, rather than any words. This was a man who couldn't NOT play the guitar. As was I, it turned out.

Subsequently Pat was far more forthcoming in the particulars of this odyssey from amnesia to mastery. In a Lehigh Valley Live interview from 2014 he said: "It was either I do something that absorbed my attention or consider suicide. I reached that level, and I chose the former and began to play with toys like a child does. My favorite toy, as it always was, proved to be the one that was beneficial to begin with and that was the guitar."

Martino says he rediscovered the playfulness of the instrument, equating relearning how to play the guitar to that of a child discovering and being fascinated with a new toy. When he is on stage, there is nothing else but the music.

"Whatever it may be that stops the play is the interruption and the flow of that child's creativity. The greatest thing about the performance, in my own evolution as a human being, is the continuity in that process," Martino said "When I play, I activate the utensil, the instrument. I'm absorbed in it and there is nothing that is desired other than the act itself."

Two decades after recording with Gil, Pat recorded "You Don't Know What Love Is" again in a trio with Joey DeFrancesco. It's instructive to hear the differences. While lovely, it's more generic. I miss the silence that the duo affords. His phrasing is far more predictable, his tone less resonant. It's devoid of the same fragility, the feeling of tragedy.

I talked to Gil Goldstein about the genesis of this recording. Apparently Jaco Pastorius was with Gil one evening in the early '70s and asked him if he wanted to play with Pat Martino, who Jaco had just met in Philly. (The mind reels at the idea of a Jaco/Martino recording.) Gil said, "Of course I would!" So Jaco said call him, here's his number. Gil was nervous. Finally he screwed up his courage, called Pat, and told him he wanted to get together and play. Pat paused and said, "Are you sure?" Jaco had told him his best strategy was to bring in a really complex composition and throw it in front of Martino. to establish his bonafides. The piece he chose was "Open Road," which opens the record, and apparently it worked. Pat was impressed.

They did the record *Star Bright* first with a full band, the duo record *We'll Be Together Again* followed. At first Gil played piano, but Pat offered that "he sounded too much like Bill Evans, which would be bad for his career." He advised moving to the electric piano. Now when one imagines a session like this, from a romantic distance, one pictures a rehearsal, a set list, a discussion of strategy. No such thing existed. They both showed up in the studio absent of an agenda, recorded the original number, then simply opened a Real Book and started playing. Gil says it was his first real arranging gig, as he took responsibility for shaping the tunes.

I asked Gil if he felt good when he was recording. Did he realize how strong it was? Not at all. "At the time I didn't think we had anything special," Gil admitted with a chuckle. Greatness is sometimes an accident, is it not? It shows up when it wishes, and all the preparation in the world cannot buy it.

The duo sound—it's transparent, raw. The Fender Rhodes oscillates, it rumbles. Gil lays a firm, foundation, free of ornamentation, as Pat, with his astonishing sense of groove, shoehorns a couple of chords off the beat, casual, playing with the pulse like a cat with a mouse. Total control and yet spontaneous, he could tear the mouse in two any moment, but he waits... much is implied rather than stated.

Later Pat Metheny told Gil that he was the "star of that record." It's an interesting vantage point. Metheny heard the discipline and focus of the accompaniment—no solos, barely any fills. There's a deep generosity in this track. It's a generosity made up of what these two men didn't play.

Danny Gatton

Harlem Nocturne

American Music (Aladdin 1975)

Danny Gatton played the guitar like his hands were on fire.

At fourteen he was already playing professionally, and at sixteen shaming men three times his age. He learned everything by ear, never read music, took almost no lessons. His mother would put on Roy Clark and tell him—Hear that? You have to be better. And soon enough, he was. A torrent of ideas poured from Danny when he improvised, as if he couldn't get them out fast enough. He could always see ahead to where a solo was going, as if he had a mental GPS, and it gave his sound authority and pinpoint accuracy.

Danny could remember hearing music in his head as an infant, as if angels were singing to him.

September 1978, The Cellar Door, Washington D.C.'s preeminent music club, and Gatton and pedal steel player Buddy Emmons are trading choruses on the song "Rock Candy." The band is Redneck Jazz Explosion, and Gatton is in peak form. It's a 12-bar blues played extremely fast, and the audience is barely stifling screams of excitement as the tension mounts, each soloist attacking the timeless progression with their own virtuosic imprint. Close your eyes and you can hardly tell where one leaves off and the other begins. Emmons uses the metal slide to dip, bend, and weave between notes, while Gatton uses the fingers of his left hand to pull off those same sounds. Both play a complex idea so fast and clean that it makes your eyes go wide. Bebop harmony running head on into country twang, pure American ecstasy, as both players pull out tricks to up the ante. You don't want it to end, it's too amazing, too much fun, like watching two Olympic sprinters. But it's no footrace—it's music.

Danny's shows were a sonic amusement park, a rollercoaster of six-string hijinks, like the beer bottle used as a slide, foam spraying all over the neck, licks that would bend and distort and create shapes you didn't think were possible, like he had seven fingers.

Except it was also incredibly serious—he was doing things that no one had ever done, making other players seem like puzzled novices. Danny was an encyclopedia of styles, effortlessly conjuring jazz, country, rockabilly, blues, rock n' roll in one solo, the seams invisible. But you never had any sense that he was showing off, or posing as a "guitar hero," because he was the most unpretentious, laid back, who-gives-a-fuck guy imaginable.

How did he make it look so easy, like he wasn't trying? I'd go into a kind of hysteria when he plugged in, early on when no one knew who he was. Young as I was, I still knew that a player like Danny wasn't coming around twice.

Those days, 1974, you'd pay $3, if that, to see him at some dump like the Psyche Delly Inn in Bethesda, Maryland. It was a greasy spoon lunch joint with a charmless music room in the back. I was seventeen, but no one carded me. His band, The Fat Boys, might stretch one tune for thirty minutes, the "Mystery Train" medley or some trifle that he turned into a rockabilly epic like "Ubangi Stomp." Danny might take three solos in one tune, all of them completely different. He'd curl his

Danny with his "Mother of Toilet Seat" Telecaster

hand over top of the neck and play upside down, then do octaves in 16th notes, get a slapback delay going, bust out the Heineken bottle, splash complex jazz chords inside a rocking blues shuffle, and finally build a ten-chorus solo on "Stormy Monday" that caused young aspirants to shout for joy.

I used to follow Gatton around Washington D.C. like a stray dog, armed with a cassette recorder. I thought I could learn to play like him, but I couldn't—no one could, and in fact that sentiment became a D.C. cliche. All the local guitar-Johnnies cycled through it, slack jaws and dazed looks all across town, the enlightenment, the hope, the despair.

The first time I met Danny was with my friend Bruce Tanous. We showed up unannounced at Danny's house, a nondescript two story cookie-cutter with a small porch in Silverton, Maryland. It was close to D.C. geographically but light years away culturally. Danny walked towards us from the garage with a raccoon clinging to his neck. He was short and stout and had thick black hair cut in the shape of a bowl. He was dressed in a white t-shirt, and black rayon pants that looked a little small, pulled up over a decent sized gut.

Gatton was busy that day, so we came back another time and walked into his guitar shop, which was part mad-scientist laboratory and part boys club. He and his partner Tex Rubinowitz ran the place, nothing pristine about it, just a lot of dust and plywood benches, and guitar parts lurking around like old engines in a junk yard. They drank beer and drilled holes in 1950s Fender Telecasters. Danny wasn't precious. He'd grab your guitar from you like a piece of meat to throw on the grill.

My best pal Jim Panek and I went all over town to see Danny any chance we could. We'd show up at Desperados or The Crazy Horse and close the joint. One summer evening we rolled up to Mr. Henry's in Tenley Circle. It was a frat boy joint where Danny was playing with his new guitarist, Evan Johns, who Jim and I both knew. We were about an hour early, and somehow, I can't recall how, we ended up in a guy's car who had about a half pound of coke in a bag on his lap. He served us generous portions with what looked like a dentist's tool, told us he'd spent his whole inheritance on coke, and didn't mind, what else would he spend it on? All kinds of trouble hung around him. He'd just gotten out of a locked ward mental facility, and while he seemed smart and had a prep-school vocabulary, he could hardly connect one sentence to the next. Jim was next to him in the front seat, nodding his head, nonchalant, very empathetic. He knew how to keep the coke coming. Out of the blue the guy hit Jim as hard as he could on the shoulder. Jim yelped, and the guy said, "OK, good, if you felt that then you can still do some more blow. When you go numb, that's time to stop."

I could barely move my jaw. I was having problems speaking, and my throat was dry as the Atacama Desert. Evan Johns walked by with his guitar, getting ready to set up, and Jim rolled down the window and warmly greeted him. Cokeman offered Evan some toot, but Evan, for whom sobriety was an arch enemy, vigorously declined, "No booger sugar for me." Jim and I were spooked by that. Evan saying no to drugs? I think we both knew it was time to leave the car. We had the sense to go inside and listen to the music, while our benefactor chose to drive off and no doubt finish the bag alone. I doubted he would survive the night. Firecrackers were going off in our heads, and Jim and I drank and drank which lowered our pulse rate, and we screamed like idiots through the whole set.

Some clubs Danny would set on fire. Others he would sit on a stool and just play jazz standards, quiet and introverted, and he might decide to challenge himself to only do chord solos for a whole set. He'd call tunes that people rarely played by Cannonball Adderly or Joe Henderson. Maybe everything would be fast, maybe all slow. Behind the circus show, interspersed in a set that included The Linus and Lucy song, or later, the Simpson's theme, was a harrowing slow blues that made your nerve endings hurt.

Enter "Harlem Nocturne," an old jazz standard he arranged that had nothing to do with speed and everything to do with timing, sustain, and lyricism. You didn't want to play it after you heard Danny's version on a good night—it was sorrowful and celebratory all at once. There are pieces that belong to an artist, like "A Love Supreme" belongs to Coltrane, or "Texas Flood" to Stevie Ray Vaughn. "Harlem Nocturne" belonged to Danny. He'd turn a Blackface Super Reverb up to about eight and make his Telecaster cry.

An enigma—a normal, aw-shucks good 'ol boy who you'd mistake for a rube— and a virtuosic, visionary sorcerer who could make the waters part in the most pitiful bar in town. He was well-read, acquainted with history, philosophy, theology—a shy, funny man with a tender heart. When his old friend and beloved keyboardist Dick Heintze finally succumbed to ALS, Danny couldn't talk about him for years without tearing up. And yet he was intensely private, not one to advertise what was going on inside.

You can't talk about Danny without mentioning his obsession with things mechanical, especially old cars. A born tinkerer, he needed to know how stuff worked. He couldn't help taking guitars apart. The idea of a vintage guitar that should be left in pristine shape would make no sense to him. He'd always look for ways to make it better. The story of the "Magic Dingus Box" almost strains belief. My pal Jim was at The Psyche Delly Inn the night it all went down. Here's what happened:

It was a three-day run. Night one, Les Paul, who'd yet to hear Danny, showed up. Les was Danny's hero, and when he introduced himself after the first set Danny lit up, he was absolutely thrilled. The next night Les showed up again, this time with a gorgeous black Les Paul Custom with gold trim, and it had a new contraption he'd been toying with, a plastic casing affixed to the body called the "Les Paulverizer." You could use your right hand to manipulate knobs to control delay times and feedback. Les gave the guitar to Danny. It's the same guitar he played on Redneck Jazz.

According to legend, Danny went into an engineering fit in the next twenty-four hours. Staying up all night he tore the Pulverizer apart, needing to see how it worked. Danny mounted a new, larger metal case on the guitar from which he could run a special cable that would link his guitar to an Echoplex (a tape-operated delay unit) and a Leslie speaker (the five-foot-tall wooden speaker used to amplify a Hammond B3 organ). Now he would be able to control the various delay sounds, as well as the speed of the Leslie rotor with his right hand. But that wasn't all. He rigged Christmas lights into the operation. With the flick of a switch Danny could make the lights randomly alternate, light all at once, or pulse in time to the music. He called it the "Magic Dingus Box."

Not done yet, Danny performed radical surgery on his amplification system. He cut open his Leslie cabinet and installed both a Fender Twin and a Fender Princeton guitar amp next to the huge Leslie woofer, wired in stereo. This monster now weighed about three hundred fifty pounds, so he put industrial strength wheels on the bottom. There were so many wires coming out of the Magic Dingus Box that he had to buy a special kind of encasement for it all, BX cable, an inch thick, flexible metal jacket. When it was done the Les Paul sounded like a Hammond organ, he'd add zany delay and looping effects like you'd hear Nels Cline and Bill Frisell do some years later—and then he'd wish you Merry Christmas.

Night three of the run all hell broke loose in The Psyche Delly as he unleashed the Magic Dingus Box.

Danny Gatton. Photo by Nancy Keener

There were two Danny Gattons. One would greet you with a smile and make you giggle, the other wouldn't speak to you; one was sensitive to criticism, one didn't give a damn; one wanted success, one wanted anonymity; one wanted to play faster than any man alive, one wanted to slow down; one wanted to make money, one spurned money; one joyous, one despondent. By the time a certain amount of fame came, along with the tour bus and the long weeks away from home, he said he was too old for it. He'd just as soon play The Crab Shack with his buddies. He had genius that brought happiness to all those who heard him, and that same genius made him miserable.

Jim told me a story about a Redneck Jazz studio recording date Danny invited him to. Danny burst through the door of Bias Studio a beer in one hand, a bong in the other. Ever the perfectionist, Danny planned to overdub some guitar parts that he, and only he, found lacking. He practically ran over to his guitar and amp, taking no time to warm up, waited for the two-inch tape to be cued while sucking on the bong, and a split second before he was supposed to come in he cast the bong down and played a screamingly fast improvised lick exactly as he'd done during the original session, but maybe even a little better.

He had reflexes the likes of which neither the engineer nor Jim could fathom. Then he did it again—and again, and then many more times. It was never good enough. Finally, he got one he liked, but he was sure the engineer had missed the timing and cut off a note.

"I got it," the engineer said.

"No way," said Danny.

"Nope, I got it,"

"No, you didn't."

"Come on and listen, then."

Danny listened and the engineer had got it, and he got so excited he started jumping up and down like a little kid, and said, "Here's your prize, you're gonna get a prize!" And he proceeded to pull his privates out of his pants and gleefully leap onto the incredibly expensive control board and prance on it for a few long moments. The engineer was aghast, and Jim was laughing so hard he almost began to cry. Nothing broke. The session continued.

The other extreme—sick of it all, he'd stop playing for months at a time and just work on cars. In the late '80s he put a shotgun to his head with his wife in the room and threatened to kill himself. His wife called Danny's parents and his dad talked him down and took the shotgun out of the house. After a time, Danny's mood brightened, and he got back into music.

I'd moved from D.C. back in 1975, so I only saw Danny on the rare occasions I went home. The last time was in the early '90s, at a jazz brunch at a Holiday Inn in Tysons Corner, Maryland. Danny played jazz on an archtop while half the room talked and ate eggs benedict. He looked hungover and unhappy. I asked for a lesson afterwards. He took a drag off a cigarette, shook his head and scowled. "I don't know what the fuck I'm doin,' how am I gonna tell you?"

In 1994 Danny rigged a shotgun into a vice on his workbench, attached a string to activate the trigger, and blew his head off. A band member had spoken with him only hours earlier and seen no signs of what would follow. I was depressed for weeks. It was personal. If Danny couldn't make it, how could I? I don't mean make it onto the cover of *Guitar Player* magazine. I mean make it as a creative human being on planet earth. It made no sense to me that someone who brought this much joy to so many others could succumb to such despair inside himself.

The joy of Danny's music still lives inside my fingers, inside the fingers of a thousand other players—some who saw him, some who didn't. He lives on computer screens and bootlegs, on little-known VCR tapes, on vinyl and CD, and now in a new movie called *The Humbler*. He lives in beat up Telecasters across the land, maple guitar necks burnished dark from smoke and sweat played on beer-soaked, ramshackle stages. He lives in the river of sound that feeds all America, currents of rhythm and melody that push away the dark veil and deliver us into light.

Roscoe Holcomb

Boat's Up the River

The High Lonesome Sound

(Smithsonian Folkways Recordings 1998)

It's useful to consider what the guitar can do that no other instrument can—that is, retune the six strings in as many different ways as imagination will allow. Holcomb tunes the guitar, G/G/D/G/B/D. He picks like he was playing banjo, a high drone string on the 5th set against a syncopated thumb pattern that subtly morphs in time as if Steve Reich wrote it. The index finger picks the melody on the four middle strings in a tangle of rhythm.

It's West African music plain and simple. Holcomb's repetitive, yet elusive picking pattern, trance-like, reminds me of a balafon or ngoni. Like some other country blues artists of the earlier part of the last century there's no real time signature, although now and then it seems like 5/4. The modal tuning uses many of the intervals you'd see in Africa, or the Blues, a Mixolydian scale that sometimes employs a flat 3 and flat 5. Holcomb's main instrument was banjo, so you can see how he might play guitar like this. And as many now know, the banjo originated in Africa.

Holcomb is open about his influence from the African American community, from players like Blind Lemon Jefferson. Maybe he was familiar with the African American string bands of the time.

Country music, of course, is rooted as much in Africa as the British Isles. Take Arnold Schultz, a Black man born in 1886 in western Kentucky. Bill Monroe credits him as influential in the development of bluegrass music. Schultz, who was never recorded, "played straight old-time music, fingerstyle blues, jazzy dance band numbers, and bottleneck ... he had a palette of chords he used to expand the bland harmonic structure of most popular music of the time."

As John Hartford tells it, "In the fall of the year Arnold would take his guitar one morning, and simply walk out of the house and into the woods and sit down on a stump and play. After a little spell of that he would pick up and move on out into the forest where he could find a stump or somewhere else to sit and repeat the performance. Thus, if you were his family on the porch of the house you could hear him disappearing out through the woods with his music. He would winter in New Orleans, and I'm sure he played music on the street, and of course this was the days of Jelly Roll Morton and his tremendous influence on all who heard him. Jelly Roll pioneered passing chords in ragtime, and you know Arnold could hear this... in the spring he would find a northbound boat, connect up the river to Evansville, and thence up Green River and come home through the woods stopping every once in a while to play some tunes in the breeze."

Schultz was one of many who barely made it into the history books.

Roscoe Holcomb (c. 1960)

There's no recorded evidence of his playing. He and Holcomb drank from the same well.

Holcomb's stew of influence is sui generis. The driving rhythm from his percussive right hand sucks you in, there's something mysterious and dark about it, it's a whirlpool, you get lost in it, stop counting one. The singing elevates the impact, a high, reedy tone like barbed wire that literally changed folklorist and New Lost City Ramblers guitarist John Cohen's life. It startled him so much he made a movie about Holcomb, and coined the phrase "high lonesome sound" to describe Holcomb's effect. Holcomb based his sound in the traditions of the Baptist Church. It is lonesome. You hear the hollows and grievances and destitution and tenacity of rural Appalachian in the Depression. You get disoriented in it, forget what century you're in.

"Boat's Up the River" is one of countless anonymous Appalachian tunes, with its roots probably up in the highlands of Scotland. Like most of these tunes its meaning is mysterious. Its ambiguity, not just the lyrics, haunt you. It could be about any loss you've ever had. The few versions you find all feature different lyrics, Olabelle Reed's for instance. The uncertainty is its strength. If a songwriter were to aspire to be Bob Dylan, they'd do well to study this song.

Holcomb was a coal miner, a construction worker, and a farmer. He died of emphysema and black lung disease. He spent the bulk of his musical life unrecorded. The next time you worry about not having enough time to practice or compose, picture working in a coal mine all week.

By the 1970s many of the rough edges, the uneven bars, the tuning, had been ironed out of country music. Compared to the sound of Roscoe Holcomb, today's radio friendly hits are smooth and clean, made for the masses. Holcomb's sound, like Robert Johnson's, feels almost frightening in its raw intensity. It's hard to find any danger in modern country music anymore. It's like a big fluffy pillow. Holcomb has more in common with Joe Strummer than Garth Brooks.

Note: The book *Hidden in the Mix: The African American Presence in Country Music* (Duke University Press, 2013) is the source for the quotes about the roots of country music.

Emily Remler

Ode to Mali

Transitions (Concord Jazz 1983)

I'd love to talk about Emily Remler from a gender-neutral position. She was a great jazz guitarist, not a great *female* guitarist. But I can't. You can't ignore the fact that in the late 1970s she was a woman in a completely male-dominated world. Gender roles at the time were such that women, by-and-large, were dissuaded from playing instruments like guitar, especially in jazz or rock settings, due to a lack of female role models and from rampant sexism on the bandstand. Multiple sources confirm Emily could outplay most contemporaries, male or female. But she was judged by a different metric—by other musicians, by record companies, and by audiences. Determined not to concern herself with what others thought, Remler vowed to work harder than anyone else, and she achieved more in her short life than most of us who live into old age.

Emily was born in New Jersey and took up guitar at age ten. While she enjoyed Hendrix and Clapton, she quickly fell in love with jazz, went to Berklee for a couple of years, and soon began playing with some of the better players on the scene. For a while Remler was based in New Orleans. Her focus was jazz standards, she played a hollow-body guitar with a clean tone. In a 1982 *People* magazine interview, she said, "I may look like a nice Jewish girl from New Jersey, but inside I'm a 50-year-old,

Emily Remler. Photo courtesy of MC Jazz and Marty Ashby.

heavy-set black man with a big thumb, like Wes Montgomery." She eventually moved back to the New York City area and began to work her way into the scene.

In the late 1970s, the great Herb Ellis championed her and she was soon signed to Concord Records. This was a big deal, Concord was a substantial label with a roster that included Joe Pass, Ella Fitzgerald, and Oscar Peterson. Her early records and live performances show a complete command of the jazz language. What set her apart, I think, was her gorgeous phrasing. Her playing is distinctly tuneful, rhythmically joyful, and buoyant. Emily was said to be competitive. She kept getting better. She never put down the guitar, she was always practicing. She had no problem hanging with the guys, had a good sense of humor, and many is the time she left her contemporaries wide-eyed after a show. She won best guitarist of the year in *DownBeat* in 1985.

Prejudice is a curious thing. There's absolutely no logic to the idea that gender or skin color might pre-determine ability. With what logic could you say that a Black man is incapable of playing country music? Black people have been playing country music for thousands of years. What do you think a griot is? A singer who tells stories about the culture and accompanies himself with a simple chord progression. Sounds like country music to me.

Of course we all know about the unremitting mistreatment of black jazz musicians throughout the 20th century. In the early '70s saxophonist Dave Liebman was shunned by members of Miles Davis' group because he was white. Dave has told me about Miles overhearing them putting him down and speaking up—"Dave has no color." What exactly would lead a man to think a woman couldn't play jazz? Thank goodness this mindset is changing.

I've seen it in action. I was at a school jam session around 1978 where drummer Bernard Purdie was the featured guest. I should first say that playing with him changed me. It was the first time I experienced the ecstasy a master drummer brings, understood what the word "groove" meant. There was a female saxophone player there, my age, 19 or 20 years old, and she was a good player. Purdie explicitly told her that she had no future because she was a woman, that a woman couldn't play jazz. She was really hurt by that. Steaming mad. I could hardly believe someone could be so cruel and stupid in a setting where encouragement was expected and required.

A lot of Emily's early work stands in the shadow of masters like Wes Montgomery. It's somewhat referential, as might be expected for a young player. She was on her way towards a more personal sound. Evidence of this growth occurs on her 1984 record *Transitions*. "Ode to Mali" steps outside the 2/5/1 hierarchy. It references West African modal music, but also contains some lovely chord changes. Here she enlists a band that couldn't help but take her into some new territory, Eddie Gomez on bass, John D'Earth on trumpet, and the incomparable Bob Moses on drums. I, too, was playing with Moses at this time, while I was living in Boston. His writing and drumming and ranting were hugely impactful. Moses had an ability to stretch you to your limits and beyond, he'd practically shame you into playing something you didn't know you could do. He was a Brooklyn-shaman-voodoo-Jew, into groove music from all over the world, and I have no doubt he colored the arrangement and feel of this tune with his strong personality.

So-called world music was starting to be in vogue, and this expanded the sense of what was possible in a jazz context, I think mostly to the benefit of jazz. I love the slinky, funky, yet spacious feel of this piece, the squeals and wails of the trumpet, the concise, groovy guitar work. Some folks I talked to say that Emily's most progressive work was her last record, *This Is Me*. I get that. With its hyper-modern production, overdubs, and more extended song forms it certainly suggests a new direction. I'm guessing some record funder wanted to make her the "next Pat Metheny," a perilous endeavor. For me, Emily's last record comes close in its production values to smooth jazz. The writing is wonderful, and her playing is smoking. But something about "Ode to Mali" appeals to me more. It feels more spontaneous, organic. Her last record was just a beginning. There's no doubt that her best work was yet to come, yet there would be no more.

Remler's close friend Leni Stern, a fellow leading light in the women's jazz guitar world, told me she and "Em" would "wear out bass players shedding standards." They drove to the sessions in Emily's dad's green Chevy whose driver side door wouldn't open, so Emily would climb through the window. After these sessions Leni and the bassist would try to drag Emily to AA meetings, hoping she would quit her heroin use. In 1990, just as they were celebrating her sobriety, Emily began touring again. She went back to using and died of an overdose in a hotel room after a gig in Australia.

You want to ask why. But the answer is no answer at all. We see it over and over again. Being a human being, being an artist, is hard work. The most blessed are often the most unguarded. Lurking insecurity, hidden doubt, or just the need to dampen powerful emotions is always a liability. The job of the artist is to reveal herself in every performance. It's easy to want to run from all that.

People who knew Emily were crushed by her death. She left a lot of love behind her. The Manchester Craftsmen 's Guild in Pittsburgh, where Remler spent some time, has expended quite a bit of energy perpetuating her legacy. In 2010, an album called *The New Promise* was released in honor of Emily, with Sheryl Bailey featured on guitar, in big band arrangements of her music. There's an increasing number of fantastic women guitarists in jazz, every year more show up at the guitar camp I run. I hope that all of them know about Emily Remler. To all of them I'll quote something Emily would often say to Leni.

"Learn not to care, no matter what anyone says."

Allan Holdsworth

Sphere of Innocence

Wardenclyffe Tower (Restless Records 1992)

"Music is so huge… I don't know *anything!*"
—Allan Holdsworth 2014

I met Allan once—between sets at the Iridium in New York City, circa 2012. Journalist Bill Milkowski introduced me as the two began to converse outside the club. Allan leaned casually against the asphalt wall as the mass of humanity sped by on Broadway. He was thin, tall, and looked with wry indifference towards the small gathering of fans around him.

Bill said, "Allan, that was an amazing set, you're on fire tonight."
"I fucking sucked."
"What? C'mon!"
"Bloody wanking."
This was, I later found out, Allan's all-too common refrain.

I wondered what to ask him. Given his self-deprecation, questions about technique seemed improvident, as did reverential platitudes. So, I inquired about the massive, churchy reverb he'd employed for a gorgeous solo chordal intro. Reverb and delay settings are quite personal to a guitarist. Some like a lot—Metheny, Terje Rypdal, while others use almost none—Jim Hall, Steve Cardenas. Bill Frisell had a period where he had a long, silky reverb, but now he frequently uses very little. There's a lot of area between to swim in. Allan's was *massive*. To me it felt inspired by the grand acoustics of European cathedrals that I imagined he'd grown up near. My question interested him. He said it wasn't reverb at all, rather a series of eight stereo delays cascaded together. He began to describe a one-of-a-kind contraption he'd built, the delays of various lengths routed through a re-purposed early Mac computer, then sent through an "AMS" unit which somehow triggered various dingles and doodles and dattles, and after nine seconds he'd completely lost me. It reminded me of calculus class in high school.

Holdsworth was an inventor. He loved beer and despaired of getting a proper British ale in the U.S. Apparently to get the smooth head of an English draft beer you need wooden casks, and in the U.S. all beer kegs are metal. Allan invented a mechanism that would attach to the metal keg, and through some sort of alchemical transformation remove the carbonation to deliver the taste and head of his beloved ales. It was called the *Fizzbuster*. To soak the tubes of his amplifiers he invented the *Juice Extractor*.

In the '80s he built a box he called "the coffin." This was an attempt to get the overdrive tone he desired without turning it up too loud. It was a 12-inch speaker enclosed in a sound-proofed box that had a Shure SM 57 microphone attached to the speaker. The mic connected to a mixer, from which he processed the sound with his delays, and that led into one of two power amps and his speaker cabinets. If you're not a guitar player, rest assured that this level of engineering detail was extremely rare. And how did he even learn to build this stuff? Allan had a recurring dream of seeing himself from the back, staring at a wall of equipment as he heard a glorious sound, and upon waking he would try to find that sound, but never succeed. He might spend the entire day of rehearsal tweaking his sound with no music played.

Holdsworth invented a new way of playing guitar. He invented his own chord voicings, his own scales, his own song forms. He was one of only a handful of people to play the Synthaxe, a space age MIDI guitar from the mid-1980s that triggered synthesizers, and which he tuned in 5ths.

He designed his own overdrives, sometimes using toaster wire, which he played in an instantly identifiable, virtuosic style. No one has even come close to emulating him. His first love was the saxophone, and he based his legato playing style on horn players such as Cannonball Adderly, Coltrane, and Michael Brecker. Imagine a basketball player regularly sinking shots from mid-court. That's Holdsworth. Allan didn't read or write music. He kidded his bandmates who needed the "little dots" to tell them what to do.

There are virtuosos and prodigies, visionaries and trend-setters. A genius is something different. A genius can't be explained. His or her ability defies logic and most laws of the physical universe and may or may not have to do with technique. A genius could practice two hours a day and be one of the greatest musicians alive, whereas someone else could practice six hours a day and not even make it onto the rising star *DownBeat* poll. The genius isn't capable of thinking like other people and seems to have arrived fully formed onto earth. This is partly an illusion, of course. Even a genius works hard and goes through a developmental stage, but it's quicker and more self-directed than most. Thelonious Monk comes to mind. Prince, Wayne Shorter. Geniuses can be notoriously circumspect about their talent. If you asked Wayne Shorter how he achieved a certain transcendent solo he might reply, "I'm just watching time go by."

When called a genius Allan would respond with a shrug that he was "no genius," he was "dumb as hell." If effusively praised he would say, "Maybe it was something I ate." He would have none of what I've just written.

Allan came up in the 1960s working in top-40 bands and he played a ton of blues. He subsequently tried to completely excise the blues influence from his sound. In the 1970s, he was a sideman in bands led by Tony Williams, Bill Bruford, and Soft Machine. He was obviously a singular talent. But nothing could prepare the listener for his breakthrough solo record, *IOU*. This was something brand new in electric music. Its epic scope and original compositional style were leaps and bounds above what he'd done before.

Around this time the powers that be decided they wished to make Allan famous. He was signed to Warner Brothers records, Eddie Van Halen was set to help him, and the acclaimed pop producer Ted Templeman was brought in. It was a disaster. Allan was supposed to wait till Van Halen was done with a tour to begin the record, however, he was impatient and brought the band into the studio with Templeman, who began by refusing to let him use his own singer. They wanted someone who was a star. Finally, Jack Bruce, the famed bassist from Cream, was brought in. But would Jack sell records? The whole thing was recorded twice with different personnel, and Allan lost interest in the effort due to creative differences with Templeman. If you listen to Holdsworth for even one minute you know that this man's priorities have nothing to do with fame. Certainly he wanted to be successful, to make enough money to live comfortably, but he had zero interest in games and pop mentality. Everyone walked away angry, and from then on Holdsworth only released records on small independent labels. None of them sold very well. He was always broke. Sometimes to fund a record he would sell his gear.

To some, Holdsworth's music sounds like pure athleticism, perhaps entertaining in the way a sports event is. It certainly has its share of "chops." He and his band demonstrate bravura technique at every turn. Their collective ability is staggering. And yet Allan purposely tried to avoid any of the jazz fusion cliches of the day, for instance fast unison lines. Unlike so many metal speed demons, Allan plays extraordinarily lyrical lines. The huge sound of the drums, the saturating sound of synthesizers are not to everyone's taste. But behind it all are beautiful, big-hearted compositions. His tone is like a violin, there's an ache to it, a questing sound, a longing. Take away the rhythm section and some songs can sound deeply romantic. At times I feel a certain sadness, or perhaps it's vulnerability, behind his writing.

Allan grew up in Bradford, a working-class mill town in West Yorkshire, England. Bradford was a depressing place, always "gray skies and rain pissing down," he said. He couldn't wait to get out of there. He was born in 1945, a war baby, raised by his grandparents. His birth father was a Canadian soldier whom he never met. Until around the age of 10 he was told that his mother was his sister. One time the band had a layover in Calgary where Allan believed his birth father lived. He found a phone book (this was the early 90s) and there was his father's name and number. He tore the page out of the phone book. Sometime later he went through the official process of requesting a meeting. However, his father denied the request.

His intricate harmony avoids cadences, he disdained dominant chords. Most of his songs have no discernible key center. They're made up of major and minor chords that work in cycles that Allan had no interest in explaining. He claimed to not know what he was doing. "It's just a load of rubbish," he'd say, "I dunno 'Jack Cheese' like you Berklee boys." He loved modulations, harmony that would change seamlessly so when an idea returned it was always different yet recognizable. He called it a magic puzzle. A recurrent theme might show up in a through-composed piece a minor third or half step up.

As a young man he never listened to traditional music, his only teacher was his step-father, a pianist, which explained his fondness for wide-spaced voicings. He was an autodidact, and at one point catalogued every scale that was mathematically possible in one, then two octaves. He saw the guitar neck as a big abacus and would visualize all available notes. Though he never analyzed any piece of music his inspirations were Ravel, Debussy, Bartok, and Stravinsky. He didn't listen much to guitar players. Allan's hands were huge, he employed huge finger stretches that yielded never-seen voicings. The only person who's come close to this kind of left-hand work is Ben Monder. Songs can change meter from bar to bar, and unlike most of his contemporaries he almost never sits on a one-chord vamp. There's a sense that everything is airborne, perhaps not even of this earth. One could employ any number of useless superlatives regarding his speed. It simply doesn't seem possible. What more can be said?

The piece I've chosen, "Sphere of Innocence," is through-composed. The structure is oblique, it's a series of verses where themes keep revealing themselves in new harmonies, as if a single idea kept reinventing itself. The chord changes are achingly beautiful, evolving, moving forward, yet feeling maze-like. When I began to learn this piece, I came upon voicings that told me to research his tuning. Ah ha! His guitar is tuned in 5ths (F,C,G,D,A,E). This gives the chords a wide, open feel and the tuning alone sets it apart from any other guitar composition. And it *is* a guitar piece. You can tell he wrote it on the instrument. The solo form is its own entity, referencing the opening but not repeating it. To me this is one of the most gorgeous pieces of music ever written for the instrument.

Listening to Allan can, for me, be draining after a while because so much information goes by. This is one reason I chose this track, because it shows a more quiet, intimate side. I suppose it's rare that a player who can shred like Allan chooses not to. It must be like driving a race car. If it *can* go fast, it *must* go fast. And what a thrill this velocity can be. As one after another impossible phrase builds towards the climax of a solo, the intensity can be overwhelming. Partly because of his astonishing technique Allan was constantly being called by journalists and fans the greatest guitar player in the world. He hated that. Once when the band approached a venue Allan noticed that the marquee called him a "guitar god." Horrified, he grabbed a cloth and erased those words from the chalkboard.

Allan's life was filled with drama. A breakup with his wife around 2000 caused a rupture that never entirely healed. He lost interest in the guitar for a few years. He began to drink more heavily, moving from beer to gin. Allan recorded only one solo record between 2000 and 2017—the year he died. He began many projects that he never finished. He might record something at night and erase it come morning. All his other late-career releases were compilations or live recordings. By 2015 he told a friend backstage after a show that he was finished. "I can't do it anymore, I've had it." He'd said such things before. But this time he meant it.

Vernon Reid once said to me "You know—life is so unfair. Why couldn't *one* of those one percenters peel off enough money to make Allan comfortable? Just write him a check, you know? I mean this was *Allan Holdsworth...*"

True—but I wonder. Would all the money in the world have brought Allan Holdsworth peace or contentment? This gentle, humble soul was endowed with superhuman traits, he cut out a solitary path, setting new standards for what's possible on the electric guitar. But happiness was as elusive as that sound he kept hearing in his dreams.

Alan Holdsworth at the Beacon Theater in NYC (c. 1978)

Blind Willie Johnson

God Moves On The Water

The Complete Blind Willie Johnson (Columbia Legacy 1993)

Blind Willie Johnson may well evoke the truth of the human condition better than any guitarist who ever lived. His sound speaks of agonies as old as the human heart as well as the balm to heal them. He was a fervent Christian evangelist, but his message was eternal and universal—perfectly summed up in "God Moves on the Water." It's nominally about the sinking of the *Titanic*—but the larger metaphor is there to see. Humans build great ships to journey through their lives, but a more powerful force exists. Things are going to fall apart. Get Ready.

It's not the words you pay attention to here. It's the texture of the music. There was never a voice like this, and precious few have ever played guitar with as many layers of emotion. It drowns you and makes you whole at the same time. Johnson's guttural voice contains more than one note. There's a similar affect with Charley Patton. I wonder if it's a holdover from an African singing style amongst the Xhosa people, where two notes are produced one tone apart while higher tones embedded in overtones are amplified simultaneously. The technique might well have traveled across the Middle Passage.

No one knows how this itinerant soul came to play music, only that in the early 20th century, this was one of the few means of employment available to a blind Black man. Johnson's main venue was the street—New Orleans, Dallas, Marlin and Beaumont, Texas. He'd stake out a spot on the corner and return day after day with a tin cup by his feet. The one picture we have of Johnson shows a well-dressed, handsome fellow. His first recording in 1927 sold over 15,000 copies, making him something of a star. His last record in 1930 sold 800 copies, after which he essentially disappeared. He recorded 30 sides for Columbia between 1927 and 1930 that have influenced countless players, notably Jimmy Page and Ry Cooder. One of his seminal pieces, "Dark Was the Night and Cold Was the Ground," was one of twenty-seven tracks that accompanied the Voyager spacecraft in 1977. This song was Cooder's main inspiration for the *Paris, Texas* film score. Johnson died destitute in 1945 at the age of 48.

"God Moves on the Water" makes you feel like two people are playing instead of one. Johnson lays out a rollicking thumb-picking groove with his right hand. There's so much going on it almost sounds like he's accompanied by a drummer. This is the magic of the early resonator guitars, they're as much rhythm machines as melody makers. His slide playing is subtle, filling in the spaces with pulls, cries, and moans that say more than words can ever say.

"Dark Was the Night and Cold Was the Ground," is a must listen for a slide player. I'm moved, too, by a very different piece on the same album, "I'm Gonna Run to the City of Refuge." This is one of the simplest guitar parts you'll ever hear—but the way he plays…it sounds like running—it's trance-like, an unbroken stream of strummed 8th notes that lifts you, puts you in motion.

After Johnson's death, music historian Samuel Charters became obsessed with learning about his life. Even so, much is lost to the mists of time. Johnson seems to have had two wives simultaneously. He died of pneumonia in 1945 after his house burned down. Blind Willie was exposed to the elements of the North Texas winter with nowhere to go, unable to be admitted to the hospital because he was blind, or so we're told. No doubt the fact that he was Black and broke had something to do with it as well.

Blind Willie Johnson (1927)

Mick Goodrick

Vox Humana

Gary Burton Quartet/Dreams So Real (ECM 1976)

Mick Goodrick resembled an Old Testament prophet when I had my first lesson with him in 1977, long hair graying at the temples that swung back from a prominent brow. He had deep-set eyes with a sharp, penetrating gaze. There were lengthy pauses between sentences, something remote in his being that contrasted to the shouting militia in my brain.

 I, like hundreds of others who walked through these doors, wanted so bad to be good. Mick wasn't there to pat you on the back. He was there to help you see your real self. In those days, his lessons were not so much about chord scales and guide tones but about object relations theory or Zen and the Art of Archery. He claimed he wanted to write a book entitled Then and the Art of Pluckery. His humor was sly and dry. Mick played a Carpenters tune on the stereo and asked me to close my eyes and sense the feeling in my arms and legs, advised doing this every day with some emotional music, prior to picking up the instrument. I later learned this was an exercise he learned by way of the mystic philosopher Gurdjieff, whose teaching he was quite involved with at the time. The point was embodiment, presence, a resource sorely lacking in the general discourse.

 "Vox Humana" is a Carla Bley composition that has an epic sweep to it. Its harmonic materials are simple, but the way she builds drama with these materials is original and unpredictable. Many guitar players I love most were deeply influenced by Gary Burton's records of this period, and Dreams So Real, which is all Carla's compositions, is one of the best. Gary loved the guitar, he was amongst the first to convincingly add rock and country influences to earlier incarnations of his band with Larry Coryell and Jerry Hahn. The two-guitar ensemble on "Vox Humana" included a new kid on the block named Pat Metheny. The rhythm section of Bob Moses and Steve Swallow was one of the finest not just of the time but of any time.

Here and elsewhere Mick's playing is understated, lyrical. He's using his fingers, not a pick, he doesn't pull notes, or step on a fuzz box. His solo has a lovely melodic arc, it grows upward and outward, peaking at just the right time. It sounds like anyone could do it, but ... I've played this song and can tell you that anyone can't. Mick's uncluttered, lucid approach was foundational for Metheny, who said that the first time he played with Mick he held that rarest of sensations—unlimited possibility. They thought about the instrument in similar ways. Rock 'n' roll was raging at the time, but Mick and Pat chose to ignore it, preferring a quiet beauty. Bill Frisell told me that, "When I showed up in Boston in 1973 Mick had a huge impact on how I heard sound. He took the legato, liquid phrasing that Jim Hall developed even further. He was the link from bebop to what lay ahead."

Mick's real forte was comping, he was advanced in the harmony department and felt that not enough players concentrated on the art of accompaniment. If you want to hear phenomenal chord work check out the duo record that Wolfgang Muthspiel did with Mick, Live at the Jazz Standard. It's a whole orchestra, two guitars made one.

I interviewed Mick for a *JazzTimes* article around 2015 and learned a few surprising things. He discovered late in life that he had a condition from birth that's sometimes mistaken for autism called the "Einstein syndrome." "People like this tend to be high-functioning and bright," he said. "[They're] involved with mathematics, have a parent who is a musician or an engineer or accountant. They make dictionaries and encyclopedias." This began to explain his exhaustively methodical approach to his instructional books, which are encyclopedias of harmonic possibilities. Mick also admitted that he'd never enjoyed performing. That's pretty extraordinary for someone who had performed hundreds of times over five decades. He retired from performing around age sixty. "Been there done that," he would say.

There are many great players, few great teachers. Despite (or because of) all his eccentricities Mick remains beloved by too many students to number. He had no method to speak of, no domineering principle, he didn't care to shape anyone to his image. His students sound completely different. Mike Stern sounds nothing like Lage Lund. Mick emphasized fundamentals that had zero sex appeal, he encouraged you to cultivate not just your fingers but your mind, your attitude— to find your own voice free of any fashions of the day. He never married. He was a singular, solitary soul who welcomed the world into his living room.

One of the random bits of advice he gave me in 1978 was to "try playing badly." There wasn't a morsel of irony. Or he might ask me to visualize mutilated teddy bears as I soloed. He was fond of saying "Don't practice too much." He knew that young men with guitars could take themselves too seriously.

Yeah—Mick was different. And sometimes annoying as hell. He seemed to be disinterested in the guitar when I met him in 1977. His tendency to lapse into the psychological rather than the musical could be frustrating. As much as I learned, I had mixed feelings about some of what went down that year. Fifteen years after studying with him I introduced myself at The Village Vanguard, mentioning he'd taught me in 1978. Sorrow passed across his face. "I apologize," he simply said, unsmiling. He revealed no more to me, so the apology sat there, a permanent question mark. Somehow, I felt like I knew what he meant, and I thanked him for apologizing. His regret was palpable.

Decades later I still think about this moment. What was he apologizing for? What made him so oblique and just plain weird when I showed up in his living room in North Cambridge? Well, maybe I should say even weirder than he was later in life. I called his close friend and late-life caretaker David Lee, the man who helped Mick when he got sick with ALS. David asked me to consider that my time with Mick came after he quit Gary Burton's group in the mid-1970s, and he was redefining who he was. Apparently, the experience of being in Gary's band had become troublesome. Mick stopped performing for a while and began to position himself as a bit of a Gurdieff guru. He led meetings at his house which I suppose were more meaningful to him than his music-making. He supposedly became a little puffed up with it all, he would do stuff like tell a student to paint his apartment as a lesson! Humble yourself to the master, that type of thing.

So maybe I got off easy. I never had to pick up a paint brush.

My timing may have been a little off, but in the end, I gained a ton from Mick. It was simple enough to adjust to his eccentricities. The information he had about the guitar was pure gold, worth working for. He mentored hundreds of players in 50 years of teaching, including some who would go on to be the luminaries of our time. He's far better known as teacher than player, but there are a few moments in his recorded output that are as lovely as any guitar playing I know.

What a year that was for me, 1978. I was in a bad place when I studied with him. My mother had died just before I moved to Boston, and I had no one I could talk to about it. I held my grief close, afraid to reveal anything. While I can't say that I had any heart to hearts with Mick, he did act as a kind of guide, pointing me inward. I was building towards a life as an artist, not just a guitar player.

Summer of 1978 arrived, and it was time for me to go back home; I planned to resume my college education after my year studying privately in Boston. In one of my last lessons with Mick he pried a little and he got me to admit that I was down. I suppose it was obvious. I probably had a whopper of a hangover; Jack Daniels was a good pal that year. For once his clinical detachment was at bay, and the distance between us narrowed. I spoke of the trauma of my mother's death, and Mick listened with complete attention. I apologized as I spoke, feeling I had no right to my sorrow when I was so lucky to be learning all this music.

When I was done he peered out the window for a few seconds, tipped his cigarette ashes into the tray and gently said. "Now, it all makes sense."

"What does?" I asked.

"You. Us. Why you're here. I'm glad you told me. This is an important time. You'll look back someday and see that."

Jimi Hendrix

Machine Gun

Band of Gypsys (Capitol 1970)

The draft, 1960s—tens of thousands of young men sent halfway around the world to a tiny country almost no one has ever heard of to get blown to bits. Blown up while smoking a "J" in a mud-soaked pit with leeches crawling up their legs, shit-soaked pants from dysentery, foot rot, and no food. 1969. Not the first or the last miserable failure of the Pentagon and the higher ups, but the only one with a draft. The musicians knew all about it, the ones who couldn't avoid the draft and the ones who did, they saw their friends come home in pine boxes, junk-addicted, or bug-eyed with fear. That's part of what made the music of Jimi Hendrix so fierce, so passionate.

"Machine Gun" is an assault on the privileged, arrogant stupidity of McNamara, Kennedy, Johnson, McBundy, Westmoreland, and all the rest of the American political and military leaders. But it's more than that, it's a cry against violence in the streets of America, a cry against racism and assassination, to "the soldiers fighting in Chicago, Milwaukee, and New York," as Jimi put it. And who are these soldiers? Maybe Fred Hampton, the Black Panther organizer killed in a police raid the year before this song was released. It's also a cry towards the anguish Jimi was feeling about the music business and the way he was being over-worked.

Pity the Genius: A Journey through American Guitar Music in 33 Tracks

Henry Threadgill, iconic composer a woodwinds player, told me this story some years ago; he also tells it in his recent autobiography, Easily Slip Into Another World. Drafted into the Army during the Vietnam War, he escaped combat for a while, by being an arranger for the army band.

"So I was pretty much doing what they wanted, writing arrangements of patriotic songs, crap, really, not creating waves, you know...toeing the line. Then one day an officer comes up to me and says, 'Private Threadgill, We have a three- star general visiting the base, we're going to give him a concert and show him the way we do things here. You'll arrange the material.'"

"Yessir," I say to him, "I'll get right to it sir."

"So, I get to working, and I'm tired of toeing the line, you know, writing all this bland music without character..." Henry paused to smile, mischief in his eyes. "So, I decide to arrange "The Stars and Stripes" my own way. See? The time comes and the band kicks in, and the general is up in the balcony looking content. I start waving my hands and conducting, and no one's ever heard anything like it, and the band is doing the best they can. We get through the piece, and it's like someone died in the room when we're done it's so quiet.

"So, at the end of the night the officer storms up to me, all up in my face, turning red, steam coming from his ears, and he says, 'Private Threadgill, what the hell do you think you're doing, who the HELL do you think you are?'" Henry was laughing as he continued.

"He yelled at me, cursed me up, down, and sideways, and said, 'It's over for you! You embarrass me by playing, that mess, that crazy nonsense for the general? You've insulted your country and the flag. Your days here are over. You are going to the front lines, private!'"

And sure enough, Henry was shipped into combat the next day, and he carried a rifle instead of a baton for the rest of his tour of duty. Now that's commitment. Risking your life over a piece of music. I hear that kind of commitment in the music of Jimi Hendrix.

At the point in Jimi's life that he wrote "Machine Gun," he's being torn in ten different directions, exhausted, over-worshipped, over-medicated, and his patience is frayed. In just a few short years he's been worked half to death, everyone around him sucking his life force for dollars. The words and the performance in the song are almost stream of conscious and to me the closest thing to a Coltrane performance that Jimi ever did. "Machine Gun" is a long rambling story, full of ghosts and demons, deepest blue, painful to listen to.

The sound is what grabs you first, the empty brooding space punctuated by aural bombs. You figure he's been listening to Miles Davis. It's an R&B riff The Isley Brothers might have concocted whose repetition works on you like a mantra. The wah wah is a 4th member of the band. When he hits a high B four minutes in it's one of the most electrifying moments of improvised music you'll ever hear, a blast of heat and light, and what follows is as close to the sound of war as three human beings can make. There are almost no notes in all the twelve minutes. An E minor pentatonic scale is the nominal material, but the real scaffold is the Stratocaster, the Arbiter Fuzzface, Univibe, and Vox Wah Wah.

I still don't think anyone's decoded what the phenomenon of Jimi Hendrix was. God knows they tried. Banal magazines still put him on

Jimi Hendrix, Dutch television show Hoepla (1967)

the cover in hopes of better sales. And his estate keeps cranking out retreads, anything they can package from the back pages of his short life. A human being like this only comes around a few times in any century. "Machine Gun" shows him as close as he'll ever get to protest. He sings, the words are tough and trenchant, but the guitar playing is the heart.

What is truly special about Jimi, here and elsewhere, is his phrasing. A million acolytes have copied his licks, but no one ever copped his phrasing. It's over, in between, and up inside the beat and the bar line, just like he talks. His breath, body, and spirit are in total alignment. When he settles into the slow burn of the groove, with the background vocals more than halfway through the performance, it gets downright scary. Part of the power is the intensity of Buddy Miles and Billy Cox. When the trio draws towards a close around 11 minutes in, Jimi plays with the whammy bar and feedback, conjuring whispers and howls. It's a message to the grifting monsters who brought the war to us, the veneer covering the lies.

Drew Zingg, a brilliant guitarist who I went to summer camp with in 1972, taught me my first Hendrix licks. We were roommates, which was providential. Age thirteen and he could already play every note of "The Wind Cries Mary" and "Little Wing." Up until then it was The Stones, The Who for me. Child's play compared to "Little Wing." It took forever to learn the Hendrix stuff, plopping the needle up and down, down and up, retaining a few more notes each time. I can picture the tiny Victrola at the end of my bed, my door closed, light coming in the second story window that looked out onto Macomb Street. Washington D.C. —the demonstrations were happening right down the road. Those days the cities were burning. When Hendrix came along the entire game of music changed. He made the rest of the field sound quaint.

Everyone's lazier now. You'll never get a million people to march on Washington because of a war. Nowadays people prefer talking about protest in their echo chamber online. Or maybe they do storm the Capitol, but they're so bug-infested with half-cocked ideas they think they'll find a storehouse of adrenochrome in Pelosi's office being administered by Joe Biden's personal Beelzebub.

Shoot— I'm probably lazier, too.

Jimmy Wyble

Roly Poly

The Essential Bob Wills (Columbia Classics 1992)

Jimmy Wyble played jazz guitar in the 1940s and '50s as well as anyone. He played country too, and was employed by Benny Goodman, Red Norvo, and Bob Wills, three of the most famous musicians of the era. He was born in Louisiana in 1922, grew up in Texas during the swing era, and came to Los Angeles in the early '50s. He started out in western swing bands before moving into straight ahead jazz. To this day there is no one who plays contrapuntally like he did, with two independent lines operating simultaneously. He turned away from the touring life early on and made the decision to teach and play for television shows in L.A. He rarely performed outside of Southern California and rarely released his own music.

    Jimmy wrote a series of guitar etudes that are brief, yet remarkably original snapshots in jazz counterpoint, spicy with dissonance, with a hint of Bartok's Mikrokosmos in them. They convincingly blend classical harmonies and techniques with jazz harmony and all but went out of print until the last decade. Playing two independent lines on guitar is very difficult, and to my knowledge he was the first to strictly focus in that direction. He performed some of these pieces, and then improvised on them, on a trio record from 1977, *Classical/Jazz – Live on Tape*. You can't find it anywhere. Almost all his other recordings are as a sideman.

The etudes are unique in guitar literature. But the track that most thrills me from Jimmy is the solo he takes on Bob Wills "Roly Poly" (as *unwoke* a song as you can find). The etudes are mostly for guitarists. This music is for everyone. All his lines in this brief masterpiece are connected, they feel composed, and yet free, they follow on one another. His feel is joyful, swinging with just enough hillbilly flavor in it to let you know he could do just fine playing with Mel Tillis. You can sing it, and want to when you hear it. His virtuosity is casual, but obvious. Jimmy had taste, he wasn't showy, though if you hear him with vibraphonist Red Norvo, who played super-fast tempos, you know this fellow could tear it up as much anyone. You can see why he got hired by the important band leaders. He was always playing the right thing, his bag of tricks deep, content to live on the sidelines, supporting the cause.

Jimmy Wyble with Red Norvo (1959)

The way that the Bob Wills band works amazes me more with each passing year, some of the happiest music anywhere, even when it's sad. It was essentially a country foundation with walls made from jazz big bands. It's one of the first two guitar bands, and to hear Cameron Hill and Jimmy harmonize is pure delight. Anyone who still believes that country music isn't woven into the fabric of jazz history is hiding under a rock. Charlie Parker loved country. Many of the formative players from Kansas City, New Orleans, and Oklahoma did too. Jimmy Wyble didn't need to *think* about melding styles, he just did it.

Besides Wills, Jimmy played with Spade Cooley who was one wild character. He was a Cherokee man whose band rivalled Bob Wills in popularity in the '40s. He was a movie star, a big band leader, and had hit records on the country charts. He got his name by winning three poker games in a row with a flush of aces. Cooley murdered his wife but was pardoned by then California governor, friend, and fellow movie star Ronald Reagan after serving nine years. He mounted a comeback concert while still in prison, and after receiving three standing ovations, he dropped dead backstage of a heart attack without finding out he'd been pardoned.

Jimmy was reluctant to talk about his tenure in the world of western swing. It was a dark time in his life when he was a drinker, and I'm guessing it almost killed him. Legend has it that he once set his music stand on fire during a gig. A story like that is almost impossible to square with the gentle, light-filled being who taught guitarists like Larry Koonse, Adam Levy, and Steve Lukather in L.A. He rarely played in nightclubs, maybe because of his dark past.

What could a guitar player be in the late '40s, early '50s? A bluesman, a country slinger, a folkie. Jazz on guitar was brand new. Charlie Christian swung the door wide. A few people stepped through to make it modern—Barney Kessel, Billy Bean, Barry Galbraith, Tal Farlow, Johnny Smith. The whole navigation system on the instrument was made new in those times. Now it's all systemized, it's in books, and classes worldwide. Jimmy was one of those figures who built the language of jazz guitar early on to little fanfare.

He stopped performing in the early 1980s to take care of his wife who had MS. When she died in 2006, he emerged to play some solo gigs, and became something of a saintly presence in the L.A. scene. Jimmy had a good word for everybody, he was ever encouraging to any player in his presence.

As a college student I studied with Jimmy for two years in L.A., 1976–1977. The first person I'd asked, Cal Collins, told me in the very first lesson that white people couldn't play jazz. So much for that. Someone, I can't recall who, recommended Jimmy. Mild-mannered, bespectacled, as kind a human being as one could find, Jimmy tried to get some shape in my playing. I knew little about jazz, less about country, quite a bit about rock, and thought I might be a cosmic singer-songwriter with a "jazz influence." Yikes. He patiently encouraged me to learn Charlie Christian licks, tried to get me to read better, and supported my roots as a classical player. He was friendly, soft-spoken. Christ almighty it wasn't 'til decades later I learned he played with Bob Wills! Did I even know who Bob Wills was? When I think of what I *could* have learned…

Jimmy was one of those unheralded musicians who works for a salary behind the scenes and gets to sleep in his own bed every night. I can still see him smiling as I walked into his Glendale studio, graying hair, slightly stooped, playing a big box Gibson. Do any of us understand how we *find* each other in life? He had what I needed, and I took as much as I could and left way more on the table.

Roy Buchanan

Sweet Dreams

Roy Buchanan (Polydor 1972)

Some years back in a show at The Birchmere in Alexandria, Maryland I played with a couple of guys who were in Roy Buchanan's rhythm section. We're talking hardcore southern Maryland. They pronounced Roy, *Raw*. Tattoos sagging from loose flesh on their arms, lined faces betraying too many nights in cheap motels. They still smoked too much, still looked pretty tough, but were still standing. Backstage at a gig like this (this particular one was a tribute to Danny Gatton and Roy) you see ten Perrier bottles to every can of beer. No one drinks anymore. All that ended years ago or else they wouldn't be here. These guys don't dress fancy, talk fancy, or play fancy—it is straight and hard. One of them told me this story:

Roy didn't trust banks, credit cards, or checks. He only accepted cash. He went on tour with all the money in a suitcase, and when he'd get to his hotel room, he'd put the bills under the mattress. One time he drank too much, got up in the morning with a terrible hangover, forgot he'd put the money under the bed, and the band drove off to the next gig. He realized what he'd done when they were hundreds of miles away. Now Roy didn't drive. That meant one of the band had to drive him all the way back to the previous gig after they got finished playing. It took all night and part of the next day—just past dawn he got the cash from under the mattress. It was about 5,000 bucks.

Roy was born in 1939 in Ozark, Arkansas, and in the early '40s his family moved to Pixley, California, a tiny town in the central valley with zero prospects for a guitar player. He described his home as a "happy place in a sad kinda way." His parents were strict Pentecostal Fundamentalists, a family that easily could have been in Steinbeck's *Grapes of Wrath*. At sixteen, Roy left home with his guitar looking for work in L.A. where he played one-nighters in country, soul, and rockabilly bands. He did a stint in the late '50s with the great R&B singer Johnny Otis. Roy said he learned a lot about how to make the guitar talk by listening to how Otis shaped his notes.

There's some wonderful footage of "Buch" with Merle Haggard from the early '60s, and there on the other side of Merle is Roy Nichols, one of the tastiest guitar players of all time, a Telecaster master. Roy created indelible instrumental hooks to Haggard's classic songs, many of them as memorable as Merle's vocals. The two Roys sound fantastic together, no surprise, because both grew up seeking inspiration from all kinds of American music, blues, jazz, rockabilly, and hillbilly. Nichols was a formative influence on countless pickers including Buchanan. "Buch" plays a terrific solo over a simple country tune, and when I say terrific, what I mean is it sounds exactly like Roy Buchanan. He pinches the strings and gets those heart-tugging harmonics, his tone sounds exactly like it did 20 years later, cutting like a band saw, making you squirm with its subtle intensity.

Roy made it to Texas where he played blues for mostly African American audiences. He traveled all over, sometimes barely making enough to eat, playing for three or four dollars, sleeping in fields, sleeping in bars, sleeping wherever he could. For a while he played with Dale Hawkins in Canada, who will be a familiar figure to anyone who knows the music of Robbie Robertson and The Band. Robertson would replace Roy in Hawkins' band, The Hawks, and credits Roy with teaching him more than anyone else what to play, and what not to play.

Roy finally settled in Bladensburg, Maryland, a suburb of Washington D.C. By the mid-'60s he heard Jimi Hendrix, and worked some of Jimi's songs into his set, slowly building the repertoire that set him apart. He began to make a name for himself. Younger players in town were in awe of him, he became something of a celebrity, and famous rockers like Jeff Beck and The Rolling Stones sought him out. Roy was notorious for declining an invitation to join The Stones after Brian Jones died. But his legend still grew. In 1971 PBS made a documentary about him which led to a record deal from Polydor.

Picture Washington D.C. and the ring of small, modest suburban towns around it in those days. Small bars and nightclubs were everywhere, Mama's Place near Dupont Circle, The Childe Harold, Strick's, The Dixie Pig, The Quonset, The Crab Shack, Desperados, The Crazy Horse, all gone now. It was a somewhat segregated place in the 1960s and early '70s, and yet musicians, as always, were inclusive and open in their tastes. You could hear the finest bluegrass on earth, by bands like The Seldom Scene and The Country Gentlemen, and soul, jazz, and funk by Roberta Flack, The Blackbyrds, Terry Plumeri, and Ron Holloway. Blues was everywhere from bands like The Nighthawks and the legendary Powerhouse Blues Band. The folk scene was going strong on the heels of people like Jorma Kaukonen, Emmy Lou Harris, and John Fahey. There were psychedelic rock groups, sometimes backed by light shows at Pipeline Coffee House or at Fort Reno with bands like Tractor, Crank, Grits, or Grin (with Nils Lofgren). A little later there were outliers like Root Boy Slim and dear old Evan Johns, who I jammed with before we started shaving.

There was, and is, a D.C. sound, or more particularly a sound from the Anacostia Delta. It's inclusive of all the above. The town occupies a unique geography, sitting plum on the Mason-Dixon line, making it both a Southern and a Northern town. Wisdom and inspiration lay in both; JFK famously said that it was a city with Southern efficiency and Northern charm. Upscale and educated mixed freely with folk and funk. Music flowed into Washington from the Blue Ridge Mountains just to the southwest, the Chesapeake Bay region of southern Maryland, and from African Americans who brought their music from the Deep South through the middle years of the century. It came down from New York and across from Baltimore, and from people from all over the world, whether working class immigrants or diplomats.

If you were a decent player in those days, you'd be gigging all week long—these days you're lucky to play once a week as a bandleader, and that's if you're at the top of the food chain. People like Roy Buchanan become who they are by playing thousands of gigs for lunatics, drunks, holy rollers, grifters, newlyweds, pickpockets, brick layers, people celebrating a wedding or a wake. It's hard to become a player like Roy Buchanan when your steady gig is playing alone to a camera in your bedroom.

Roy was shy, introverted, uneasy in social situations. He spoke with the guitar. When you talked to him, he wouldn't look you in the eye. One musician who was in the scene at that time theorized that he might have been on the autistic spectrum. When it came time to play there were no words. He'd start a tune and expect you to fall in line. He had no sense of hierarchy in music. He'd just as soon play the jazz tune "Misty" as a rockabilly thumper.

In a lot of YouTube clips of Roy on stage, he doesn't look particularly happy. He looks serious, intent, he's tall, stoic, with shaggy hair and a beard, looking like he stepped out of a Bible story. Roy was born again. Sometimes during a break when fans would gather around him, he'd start to lecture about Christian values and the Messiah. He had an edge to his chin when he leaned in to play the blues—you could feel the weight of the notes. Part of the weight was that sound, another D.C. Tele player with that Fender Telecaster Blackguard thing. He used to take a Fender Vibrolux, which is a loud piece of machinery, turn it towards the back of the stage so it wouldn't make him deaf, put a microphone in front of it, and crank the volume to 10. He didn't need pedals. It was blue collar music from southern Maryland, instrumental music with little commercial potential, played as if his life depended on it.

A little-known fact—Danny Gatton played a few gigs on bass with Roy in spite of the friendly rivalry they had. Supposedly, if Gatton and Buchanan both had a gig the same night they would call crosstown and ask the bartender to leave the phone off the hook so they could hear what the other was doing.

In the early '70s, there was the Roy camp and the Danny camp, and you'd get into arguments. It was like some fans being for Clapton and others being for Hendrix. The truth is they were completely different even if now and then they would do dead-on impersonations of each other. Bassist Pete Van Allen, who played on "Sweet Dreams," is one of the few people to have played on stage when both were playing guitar. He told me they tried mightily to outdo each other, it was a hell of a cutting contest, and some of the best fun he's ever had in his life.

Pete turned me onto a great bootleg that was made in those days, around 1972 by the group Roy called The Snake Stretchers, the same group that recorded "Sweet Dreams." Their version of Neil Young's "Down by the River" is on fire.

I suppose Roy was one of those tough guys who keeps it all inside. It makes the tenderness in "Sweet Dreams" all the more poignant. The tough guys don't bend, they break. You hear sorrow and triumph in the searing melodies. I saw Roy play only once at the Roxy in LA. Not being a hardcore blues fan, his music wasn't as important to me at the time. He didn't look like he wanted to be there. He played a slow blues that went on and on and on. It was towards the end of his life and God only knows what was going through his mind. How I wish I'd seen him on a better night in some dive in D.C.

Roy Buchanan
Pinecrest Country Club, Shelton, CT

But "Sweet Dreams"? It's Roy at his finest. It's a pretty lullaby written by Don Gibson in 1955. Who could have imagined the transformation it underwent? Roy brings startling gravity to it—he states the aching melody with string pulls and vibrato, and uses top-of-the-neck cries, fast flourishes, and subtle picking techniques to tell a moving story. There's seismic content in just a few notes. Pete Van Allen said it was done in one take. There's a good reason that Jeff Beck dedicated "Cause We've Ended as Lovers" to Roy Buchanan. Roy is all over Jeff's track. You've got to go through Roy to get to Jeff.

Roy used to complain that record companies and producers were always breathing down his neck telling him what to do. He vowed to quit recording in 1981 but was coaxed back into making a disc for Alligator Records in 1985. He claimed this was his only record where he had total artistic control. He continued to tour, but his career wasn't building. No doubt he was weary of 30 years of one-nighters. At some point he was taking classes to be a barber, figuring music couldn't last.

Like so many others, Roy had problems with drugs and alcohol. On and off he took speed, black beauties, other kinds of pills. In 1988 he was arrested for domestic abuse and put in the Fairfax County jail. He was found the next morning hanging from his shirt which was tied around a metal pipe. Another inmate in the jail at that time swore that he saw Roy's face bruised, as if he'd been beaten. Who knows? Whatever happened, it was a godawful way for this marvelous soul to leave the earth.

There's a quote of Roy's from the PBS documentary that haunts me. He's talking about his life in music: "I can remember some lonesome times, alright. I think the lonely thing is kind of born inside a person. That's what makes him play. Your soul seems to be completely someplace else from other people. My dad called it the blues. I think he was right."

Want to learn to play like Roy Buchanan? Study that.

Snoozer Quinn

Lover Come Back to Me / On the Alamo

(1948)

Snoozer Quinn was described by contemporaries as the best guitarist they'd ever heard, yet much of his life and career are a mystery. Snoozer, born Edward, flourished in the late 1920s, slowed to a crawl by the late '30s, and died of tuberculosis in 1949 at the age of 42. The only recorded evidence of his work are a handful of tracks cut to acetate in a hospital room just a few weeks before he died.

This track, "Lover Come Back to Me / On the Alamo" is found on some compilation albums such as *The Magic of Snoozer Quinn with Johnny Wiggs and Johnny Wiggs Big Five*, released in 2014 and available on YouTube (youtu.be/OKsMtevAyHA). As endearing as these tracks are, we can assume they don't capture the best of what Snoozer had to offer. For that we are left with our imaginations and the testimony of his long-dead contemporaries. Other tracks were recorded for the Victor label, but no masters survive. Most of what we know about him comes from brief newspaper clippings and the oral histories of musicians of the time such as Frankie Trumbauer and Johnny Wiggs.

Snoozer lived most of his life in Bogalusa, Louisiana. As a child he showed uncommon aptitude for music and quickly learned to play piano, violin, banjo, and then guitar. He was mostly a finger-style player, doing arrangements of the popular tunes of the time in a swinging, orchestral manner that linked country blues with the jazz that was being invented in New Orleans. It's said he played virtuosic single lines with a pick, too, but none of that made it to record. The vagaries of time don't allow us to separate fact from fable, but breathless accounts of Snoozer in his prime allege that he could play multiple parts at once with one hand. He'd shake your hand without stopping the music. His nickname came because he played so well he seemed able to do it in his sleep. He'd wake up and start playing and play until he fell asleep. Louisiana governor Jimmie Davis claimed to have seen him walking down a Baton Rouge street in 1931 playing Tiger Rag with the guitar on his back. In the recordings from the sanitarium the guitar seems to be tuned down to a low C. Why, we'll never know.

At the age of 18, Snoozer began playing in territory bands throughout the South. The lifestyle didn't suit him. He was a fragile man, born with a cranial deformity, the left side of his head was indented from forceps used at birth. He was retiring and shy. He'd try to hide in the background on stage, hoping not to be seen. Snoozer's big break came when the famous bandleader Paul Whiteman hired him in 1928, and he spent a year in New York. The gig brought him no joy. Apparently, Whiteman gave him little space to play in the actual orchestra, rather he asked him to stroll around the tables during breaks. He was a so-called "intermission player." Whiteman would drag him to after-parties and show him off. Some of this may be because Snoozer was an orchestra unto himself not so much of a section player. He was called a modernist, a progressive. In a way he was over-qualified for the gig.

And what was progressive about Snoozer's playing? First let's consider that in the 1920s there weren't many guitar players outside of the blues and hillbilly idioms. Jazz harmony on the guitar was new, most bands had a banjo or tenor banjo, not a guitar. Snoozer would have had to be familiar with ragtime, Sousa-type marches, light classical music, as well as the country music of his region. He wasn't your typical background rhythm player, he could solo, too, and if needed he'd play the bass, chords, and melody all by himself. This was virtually unheard of at the time. We can gather, also, that he was expert at the art of small group accompaniment, connecting the dots in the harmony, providing strong support, and he most likely knew a thousand songs. Legend has it that if he started to improvise, he'd be into the tenth chorus without repeating himself.

Word got around New York, and everyone wanted to hear him. Eddie Lang, Karl Cress, and others would follow Snoozer to his hotel room after the Whiteman gig and keep him up all night asking to hear him play. Snoozer wrote home that, "They wouldn't let him sleep." Snoozer quit Whiteman's band and went back South playing mostly local and regional dates, parties, and smaller shows. Tuberculosis and booze began to rob him of the ability to perform by his mid-thirties.

There are pictures of Louis Armstrong playing with Snoozer. We know that this was an era of extreme segregation, and that plenty of prejudice against Black musicians existed. Still most jazz musicians never cared much for that. Great musicians found each other, race be damned. I wonder what African American guitarists Snoozer was most influenced by. He was a white guitar player, but the Black traditions of the time are all over his sound—ragtime, the steady quarter note bass line in the thumb, bluesy string pulls.

New sounds perpetually emerge from the unconventional ways artists like Snoozer bring traditions together. The story of 20th century American guitar music is multiplicity leading towards unity. The artists were integrated way before the rest of society. In Snoozer's sound you hear an early prototype of that integration.

Note: The book *Snoozer Quinn: Fingerstyle Jazz Guitar Pioneer* by Dan Sumner & Katy Hobgood Ray (Out of the Past Music, 2022) is the source for many of the facts detailed here.

Sister Rosetta Tharpe

Guitar Solos

undated

From today's perspective it's hard to imagine how radical Sister Rosetta Thorpe was. She challenged every norm, defied all odds. She was an African-American woman guitar player in a completely white male dominated business, she was bisexual, her career swung between the music of the church and the music of the nightclubs, and all of this in the 1930s and '40s, an era in which any one of these things might have defeated her.

Born in Arkansas in 1915, by the age of four Sister Rosetta was singing gospel at her mother's side in the Pentecostal church. She took up the guitar, and it immediately became clear she was a prodigy. In the mid–1920s the family moved to Chicago where she was exposed to blues and jazz, and soon she was blending it all with her gospel chops. Her secular music scandalized her church audience, but she developed a huge following in the '30s and '40s. So great was her popularity, that in 1951 twenty-five thousand people paid to attend her wedding (her 3rd marriage) to her manager Russell Morrison.

Tharpe's recordings don't tell the whole story. Live clips available on YouTube suggest the truth of her explosive presence that's harder to detect on the 78s and LPs. I couldn't settle on a single tune, so I chose a collection of her solos that demonstrate her range. (youtu.be/gELe5Rj_tXU) The first thing you notice is her voice, it's huge, it smacks you in the face. Her presence is radiant. You can see why Little Richard was enamored of her, she owns the stage, parading and strutting about, throwing in a grimace and sly smile as she blasts out a groovy guitar lick. The way she inhabits the instrument reminds me a little of Jimi Hendrix—it's not an appendage, it's part of her body. Everything she does is a dance. She employed a number of guitar techniques to great effect, long slides up the neck, quick, almost country-like runs down below, string-pulling, banging out big chords on an open-tuned, semi-hollow body instrument. She had her own sound, a raw combination of blues, early jazz, rockabilly, and the gospel wail and shout that would soon be labeled rock 'n' roll. And what about that three-pick-up white Gibson SG she employed after 1961! A beauty.

Sister Rosetta Tharpe (1938)

This locomotive of a woman belongs in the rare club of performers who play great and sing even better—Glen Campbell, BB King, Bill Monroe. The only station above that are those freaks who *also* write great songs—Vince Gill, Stevie, Prince. If you don't know any better, you might think her licks sound dated. But you have to imagine this guitar sound arriving in the world for the first time. Sister Rosetta was an innovator, not just in her guitar work, but in her entire life story.

Imagine being under a tent in a huge field in Alabama in July 1941, sweat pouring off you, thousands of country people all dressed pretty, shouting, swaying, going into seizures from the spirit. Sister Rosetta is singing about the Lord, and then she rips into a guitar solo, crows gather at the edge of the tent, the old ladies fall to their knees and chant Oh Mercy, and a thousand alleluias echo off yonder mountains.

You hear the Mississippi country blues she was born into, the urban blues of Chicago and New York (where she moved in the '40s.) There are elements of early jazz from pioneers like Eddie Lang, the jump music that Cab Calloway and Louie Jordan made popular. But something else sets her apart—the way she strikes the strings, the force of her rhythm chops, suggests the abandon with which folks would play decades later. I'm not talking about the precise elegance of somebody such as Jimmy Nolen or Wah Wah Watson. More like the squall of Marc Ribot or Pete Townsend. The velocity of her groove makes most other guitar players sound polite by comparison. Even when she's backed up by a large jazz ensemble led by Lucky Millender, she seems to be the one driving the band.

She represents one of the great wonders of our time—this exultation emanating from one of the most marginalized, exploited, and wronged group of people in the history of the world. She offers gladness to all, even her oppressors.

Instead of adopting the girlish personality that was prevalent for women in show business at the time, she developed an outrageous personality. Sister Rosetta was determined to better any man, she was a prankster who loved to make people laugh, deflating any notions of how a woman was supposed to act. Male guitarists, not used to being outgunned, were in awe of her. They said, "she plays like a man," their way of offering a back-handed compliment. Tharpe never thought of herself as a "woman guitarist" and never seemed to suffer from lack of confidence around anyone.

For a few years between marriages, she lived with her performing partner, Marie Knight. Rumors circulated about their relationship, but judgments didn't sway her. Nor did the racism of the time. When she toured with an all-white gospel group, The Jordanaires, she stayed in the tour bus in the small towns of the South while the others dined in segregated restaurants. They relentlessly worked across the country, sometimes doing more than one date in a day. Her marriage to manager Russell Morrison was something of a puzzle. Friends felt he was beneath her, that he was more interested in her money than anything else. The relationship appeared more transactional than romantic, and towards the end of her life, when she had a leg amputated because of diabetes, Morrison kept pushing her into performing so the money would keep flowing though she was debilitated and exhausted.

Imagine some collaborations if Sister Rosetta were alive in this century. The "godmother of rock 'n' roll" seemed capable of anything, an album of jazz standards with Wynton Marsalis' band, or a duo with Springsteen, Brittany Howard from the Alabama Shakes, or Whitney Houston. Prince and she had a lot in common. Seems to me her view was an unlimited horizon.

In the 1950s Tharpe's popularity began to wane. She swung back and forth between recording gospel and pop, unsuccessful in catching the attention of the record-buying youth. She became part of the blues circuit in the '60s, but much of her popularity still came from her rabid gospel base who forgave her forays into secular music. By that time, other performers like Ray Charles had also begun to break down those walls. British blues players, who borrowed most of what they knew from her and her brethren, snapped up her audience. Sister Rosetta's diabetes brought on a stroke in 1970. She passed in 1973 at the age of 58. Her gravestone read: "She would sing until you cried, and then she would sing until you danced for joy. She kept the church alive and the saints rejoicing."

David Lindley

Call It a Loan

Hold Out (Jackson Brown 1980)

Sometimes I picture the greatest party I never went to—a ton of smart, funny people, no one blabbing about themselves too long, incredible food spread over multiple tables, sun going down, every glass of beer or wine tastes better than the last … and a guy is playing over in the corner who knows every fine song you can think of, none of the usual boy scout crap, and a bunch more you never knew—it's David Lindley.

He's dressed in pink polyester pants, a paisley polyester shirt, two-tone shoes and mismatched socks. His sideburns have more hair in them than my whole head. Every last note he plays is perfect. Not exact, mind you, not according to any book you've read, not the notes that won the award, or got anyone rich. The right notes. This fuzzball musters up Mississippi John Hurt, a Scottish reel, a bouzouki tune from somewhere-istan, kinky funk by Little Willie Johnson, a Link Ray B-side, some Laurel Canyon dreamers, a Warren Zevon rocker, ska, a children's song from Zambia, a quadrille from Madagascar, and an Algerian resistance anthem. Plus, he's funny.

Lindley played on more records than most people own, but I'm guessing few people under forty have even heard of him. He played banjo, guitar, hardingfele, cumbus, mandolin, cittern, oud, charango, lap steel, Weissenborn, violin, zither, and more. But here's the thing that can't be quantified, the thing no one can teach you, and it has nothing to do with how much or how little you own or know. He knew *what* to play. His guitar parts were perfect miniatures, always adding just enough and never too much. He had time, tone, and touch, and always played for the song, not himself. He prized *sound*. Like Ry Cooder, who he inspired, he was a total retro gear head, and knew about the under-the-radar guitars and pieces of guitars that were fabulous—and used them to great end.

A true folk musician. Or maybe a *folks* musician, because there were a lot of folks inside him.

Lindley's first instrument was banjo. In the early- and mid-1960s he won the local Laurel Canyon-based banjo competition so many times they banned him. From banjo he blasted outward into just about everything. In that he was similar to his Californian contemporary Jerry Garcia, also a virtuoso trad banjoist in his youth, who soon began to pursue more progressive ideas. Jerry was mostly into jug band and mountain music; Lindley knew that stuff but also expanded into flamenco and Middle Eastern music. His father had turned him onto music from around the world in his youth, and he developed a particular love of Persian classical traditions. There's a remarkable clip of his late '60s band, Kaleidoscope, where Lindley plays an oud in a rock 'n' roll context. That group is a zany window into the flower power sound, those few years when bands like Jefferson Airplane, The Zombies, and Quicksilver Messenger Service began to dress in bellbottoms and paisley, crank it up, thrash mightily, and write LSD-inspired lyrics.

Lindley became a go to studio ace in countless '70s California sessions—Dylan, James Taylor, Graham Nash, Linda Ronstadt, and Jackson Browne. His moment of fame was probably the slide solo he takes on Jackson's "Runnin' On Empty." He has unique tone, great intonation, it's tuneful, hummable, with just the right level of passion. But I've chosen another track, a duo he did with Jackson, "Call it A Loan." Apparently, this was an instrumental piece he brought to his pal who then added lyrics. It's simple and lovely, it tugs at the heart without being maudlin. It's a small, impactful package that comes from everywhere.

I'm sad to say I slept on Lindley. I'm trying to figure out why. I only saw him play once, a duo with Ry Cooder. This was a guy I should have

David Lindley

David Lindley in concert with Ry Cooder, Brisbane Australia (c.1980)

hunted down. I even lived in the same town as him when I went to college in Claremont, California. Henry Kaiser told me that Lindley was "the best musician I ever played with." He had impeccable time, and command over a crazy number of instruments. When Lindley lost interest in being a sideman in the '80s, he started his own band called El Rayo X that was kind of a reggae/rock/ska party band in which he was lead singer. Again, he was out in front of the times. Reggae had just entered the American blood stream. He went on to make fifteen solo records on all variety of axes and continued to search for new sounds and collaborators. Most notable to me was the incredible work he and Kaiser did in bringing Malagasy string music into American consciousness on the Shanachie label.

His decision to go solo, rather than, say, sign onto tours with his famous allies, is interesting. He wasn't really a composer—and not the most charismatic singer. Without one or the other any sort of real success was unlikely. Obviously he didn't care. His choice to move almost exclusively to acoustic instruments in the 2000s came about after sustained exposure to feedback from stage monitors that damaged his hearing.

He loved a lot of things, and did a lot of things, and was fine staying out of the spotlight.

I wonder—do studio musicians like David even exist anymore? Not many. Because the ability he accrued from a very young age has little purchase in today's recording kingdoms—someone who has this breadth of instrumental facility, technical chops, the ability to know exactly what each part should sound like, someone who can own a song without being in the spotlight. And offer ten different string instruments as options. He made hundreds of other people's records sound better. Not content in that role he struck out on his own. Highly educated, diligent in protean traditions, eccentric, full of curiosity, and supremely soulful.

"Thumbs" Carllile

Springfield Social Club

Tennessee Guitar (Starday 1962)

The universe never gets bored. Right when you think you've seen it all—you haven't. Scientists estimate that there are 8.7 million species on the planet. How many have you seen? Maybe a thousand? The world is profuse, fantastic, unknowable, and the imagination infinite. Some people stretch the limits of the mind, others the body. You rarely get both.

    Kenneth "Thumbs" Carllile grew up in poverty on a tenant farm in southern Illinois. Legend says his sister had a dobro resonator guitar that he liked to play as a child. She stole the slide from him (the metal bar used by the left hand to engage the strings), and so he decided to play the left-hand notes with his thumb. More precisely he sat the instrument on his lap and positioned his left hand to fret the notes as if he were playing piano. He picked with the thumb of his right hand and his index finger. Supposedly his hands were too small to wrap around a conventional neck, so when he finally got an electric guitar, he stuck with his singular technique. It's the damnedest thing. Go on YouTube right now and look (youtu.be/7RxceN0cyRk). It's as if this reed-thin cowboy dropped down from Neptune. If this were just a parlor trick it would be one thing, but he's a top tier player.

    What is it inside a person that motivates them to be different from everybody else? Most of us are content to stay in the crowd, keep it safe, or at most be a *little* different. Why stick your neck out? Convention is magnetic, it motivates and surrounds every part of you from the moment you're born. Most of the advertising we're subjected to convinces us that we should be like everyone else, listen to the best-selling tracks, dress in the best-selling clothes, believe the platitudes of failed leaders. So, here's a guy who decides he can make a living playing the guitar in the 1950s in the middle of nowhere, which is crazy enough, and then he decides to do so with his thumbs. It makes you want to stand up and cheer.

It's said that Thumbs was kicked out of high school at around age 16 for refusing to shave. Refusing to shave? How is it that get you kicked out of school for that? It's the late 1940s, you're in a podunk farm town, most of the men have just come back from war, they're exhausted, afraid, they think the commies are about to take over, they're about to put Ike in office, and all anyone wants is for things to be calm, peaceful, normal. Along comes a guy who refuses to shave. Out with you, you radical commie! If a guy is willing to get kicked out of school over a few whiskers you know he's got guts. He doesn't give a damn what anyone thinks. This attitude worked fine for Thumbs, he immediately started working with the country star Ferlin Husky, and then Little Jimmy Dickens saw him perform at the Grand Ole Opry and snapped him up into his band.

The track I've chosen here, "Springfield Social," is some of the best entertainment you can find. It's from the 1962 multi-artist compilation LP, *Tennessee Guitar* on the Starday Records label. The bandleader Bill Wimberley does a roll call of all the most famous guitarists of the day, and Thumbs shows how each of them plays in a succession of 8-bar choruses. We hear dead-on imitations of Jimmy Bryant, Speedy West, Chet Atkins, Hank Garland, Les Paul, and more. It's hilarious. Carllile plays anything he wants, he's got great time and feel, and a rapid-fire execution that stands out even amongst some of the big dogs of the day. Carllile recorded with Les Paul in the early '60s, and he played with country star Roger Miller for five years between 1968 and 1973. He's said to have made a solo record entitled *Walking in Guitar Land*, but I can find no evidence of it. In fact, I found little evidence that this man existed in the latter part of his life save for a 1973 solo effort entitled "On His Own" which is a blend of country licks over stodgy funk grooves.

The Wrecking Crew is in the rhythm section. File under the "nice try" department. Carllile was not a composer, he stayed fairly close to the conventions of his time. Beyond this one solo outing there's little in the way of recorded documents of Thumbs between 1973 and 1986. He's all but disappeared. Were it not for a passing conversation with the great guitarist Russell Malone I'd have never discovered him.

"Thumbs" Carllile / Hank Garland

There's a tradition of people approaching the physical mechanics of the guitar in new and unusual ways. Stanley Jordan taps the neck of the guitar with his right hand as he frets with his left (no thumb included). Stanley was, I believe, the first to play this way full-time, and to amazing effect, notably in the jazz realm with its attendant, thick harmony. Another anomaly is Charlie Hunter. In the early '90s Charlie developed the ability to play bass and guitar at the same time with an eight-string electric built specially for him. I recall seeing him early in his career in the San Francisco Bay area, baffled by the athleticism. You just can't imagine how hard it is. I guess Charlie didn't want to have to pay a bassist! Then there's Phil DeGruy in New Orleans who added numerous sympathetic strings to an 8-string axe, calling it a harp guitar.

One other important figure is the brilliant Michael Hedges. Michael did some of what Stanley Jordan did but on acoustic guitar. Using open tunings, he tapped with his right hand and used the resonance of the acoustic to create a delicious ringing effect. He'd hit the body of the instrument like a drum, and the percussive sounds gave the illusion that there were two people playing. Unlike Thumbs, Hedges was a composer, and he inspired a small legion of acolytes and imitators. Part of it was his good looks, the flowing locks, the dynamic, showy stage presence, and the deal with Windham Hill records, an acoustic label with a huge and improbable presence in the 1980s.

In 1987, Thumbs Carllile was set to open for Michael Hedges on a big tour after recovering from colon cancer. Right before the tour Thumbs died of a heart attack at the age of 58. Hedges became a legend, Carllile a historical foot note. Only a few years later Hedges died in a car wreck while driving home to Mendocino on Route One.

You can't make sense of it.

Prince

The Ride

Crystal Ball (NPG Records 1998)

With Vernon Reid

The putative subject in my conversation with Vernon Reid was Prince. However, the discussion, like many discussions with Vernon, became delightfully discursive. By the end we had touched on several great African American electric guitarists, not just Prince. Vernon is so informative, so smart and funny, so thoughtful, that the conversation might have gone on all day.

We know Prince was a genius producer and songwriter, a consummate showman, and fabulous singer. But Vernon and I both wondered if enough attention has been paid to his extraordinary guitar work. The parts he created are always perfectly nested in the rhythmic array, he has a kind of ruthless control over time and space. Whether Prince is being funky in the style of Jimmy Nolen, more new wave, riffing off Curtis Mayfield, or doing Hendrix-like fills, the playing is fierce, focused, dazzling. If you listen to "The Ride," either the recorded version or a live version on YouTube, you realize that his soloing is as powerful and soulful as any player of the era. It's downright ecstatic. Had Prince decided simply to be a roadhouse blues guitarist, or a session player doing rhythm parts, he still would have been successful. His tone is

Prince at Coachella (2008)

like a blast furnace, the band includes some of the best musicians in the world, and the lyrics are nasty, sexy, and just plain fun. You can hear Jimi's influence, but Prince's blues playing is all his own. A major part of it is his saturated, huge, almost metal-tinged guitar sound. It's interesting to contrast this piece with the Willie King track "I Am the Blues" (page 119). Both pieces are one chord boogies, reaching back to the earliest blues shuffles pioneered by formative figures such as John Lee Hooker, Bukka White, Son House, and Lightin' Hopkins. Willie is laid back, he's playing country blues, he's subtle and deep, while Prince is outrageously over the top and virtuosic and decidedly urban.

As we talked, Vernon referred to other great Black rock guitar players who formed a lineage leading up to and beyond Prince. And he pointed out that it had all been founded upon those blues legends listed above. Eddie Hazel who was part of Parliament Funkadelic early on, was one. His solo on "Maggot Brain," off the first P-Funk record, is a touchstone. When the track was released in 1970 it was a moment in guitar history where a lot was going on. Hendrix had just died, new and important players were popping up all over the place. Hazel's relatively short tenure with George Clinton is easy to overlook, but he had a big influence on a lot of young listeners, including Prince.

I decided to leave this essay in its original interview format in order to most faithfully transmit Vernon's words.

Note: When I spoke to Vernon, Jann Wenner, founder of *Rolling Stone* magazine, had just published *The Masters*, a new book of rock 'n' roll interviews that included only white men. He defended the book by claiming there were no Black or women rock guitar players articulate enough to merit inclusion. I knew Vernon would have something to say about that.

Vernon Reid: I've been kind of caught up in this this this whole thing about Jann Wenner and *Rolling Stone* magazine.

JH: Yeah. I knew you were on that.

VR: We're talking about articulation and this whole notion of who is considered to be worthy. And last night somebody posted a video of Hendrix playing "Machine Gun." You know?

JH: *That* video?

VR: I just found myself watching the whole clip and it's still one of the most astonishing electric guitar ensemble performances of all time. It's freaking uncanny. It literally is. What the old guys used to say is you need to tell the story with your guitar. You need to tell a story. And I couldn't fathom at the time I was first told that what it meant to tell a story. I'm thinking chords and scales and da da da. I'm trying to get my shit together, and I didn't know what these dudes were talking about. Maybe your access to narrative is such that you've witnessed enough dis-assemblage, or what have you, that you can actually pretend to tell a story, but your access to nonlinear space and understanding is such that you don't get it. Because that notion of translating the things that we do into narrative, into a story—that *leap* is the difference. That's the thing that changes. So that people who don't know anything but love music are moved—and will know the difference. And this is one of the most fascinating aspects of music as an experiential event. The spirit of the times was alive in Jimi's hands through the amp.

If you just hear it on record, you experience it as one thing. But if you look at the video, there's one moment where he's playing, and he's holding the bar. You know, he's holding the bar and doing a kind of hammer on thing, and it's becoming this wailing. The guitar becomes this kind of electric ululation, right? And he gets the smile on his face. He's suffused with joy. He's happy in this particular moment. That combination of joy and horror. It's almost unspeakable. But there it is. it's cinematic. It's orchestral and it's operatic. And it's something most definitely transmitted to Prince.

JH: Prince is of that lineage, yes?

VR: Yeah, there's no better rhythm playing. But one of the great soloists, too.

JH: It comes in part from Jimmy Nolen.

VR: Well, yeah.

JH: I'd love for you to talk Prince, as a rhythm and as a lead player.

VR: Interestingly enough Prince and I are the same age, we were born in 1958. When I would listen to Prince or when I'd see Prince, I'm acutely aware of the fact of what he heard. The same music that I heard at the same time. So he heard Mahavishnu. Santana was a big influence on Prince's phrasing, as much as Hendrix.

Another guy of that time who told a story was Eddie Hazel. I would go to "Maggot Brain," from Funkadelic. George Clinton told him, "I want you to play as if your mama died. How would you feel if your mama was dead?" And Eddie completely channeled the despair, the grief. The loss. It's really a kind of Gospel, playing over the slow arpeggiated chords and what he unleashes. He doesn't play like Hendrix at all. He doesn't imitate. He inhabits his own space. And this is incredibly important. Hazel plugged into his own emotional matrix and told his story. And this is the supreme challenge when there are dominant players that take up a lot of space in the imagination, not just of the public, but everybody, right? He was available to his own experience, his own imaginal space. You know, these feelings can be completely devastating. Our society with its norms and strictures. He was able to connect to a verisimilitude of life.

George Clinton genuinely was moved. The times I've spoken to George about it, he was genuinely moved by the Summer of Love of '67. Music was at the center of the culture. I mean, all the things were happening with painting and theater. But music was kind of a central marker of your belief systems. What were you, what did you believe with your tribe? Prince knew those P-Funk records for sure.

JH: I want to take this back to Prince because he's the next generation. His first record comes out in 1978.

VR: Prince could do *anything*. "When You Were Mine" was such a great track. On a new waveish kind of vibe, because that's the thing—he dipped around. It was very much a kind of post-punk new wave type of track. And I just loved the spareness of the guitar sound, it's almost a rockabilly vibe, you know, and the way he played those chords, a lot of fifths. It just dovetailed so well with the lyrics. It's really a song about regret.

JH: What Prince was able to do, Stevie Wonder and others too, was take a feeling like regret and somehow combine that bittersweet flavor with a sense of physical celebration.

VR: Yeah. There are two things always going on. When we have funerals, we also have a feast.

JH: Well, let me ask you this, because you started out talking about Jann Wenner. I wonder in the context of Prince, Eddie Hazel, and Jimi, in your own life, who else was important as a Black rock musician? And why is the subject crucial?

VR: Well, part of it is … the thing that we're prepared for is the way for racism to hide. The most obvious manifestation is the Klansmen in the white robe. But the central component of white supremacy is the idea of always being central. You're the one that matters. And our decisions define the age, who we are and what we choose. It pertained to the culture of music, commercial music, popular music. That central idea is that *we* define the culture. *We* define what it is. We tell you who you are. We assign your role. And your role is to inspire me. And Eddie, Jimi, Prince would have none of that. Nor Ernie Isley or Dr. Know. Others were Sonny Sharrock and Michael Gregory Jackson. All of them were amazing musicians and fell further below the radar than they should have. Racism wouldn't survive if it was always hateful and mean. It hides. The Jann Wenner thing is far more subtle.

JH: Was there resistance in the Black community to Black people playing rock music early on?

VR: It was about who would promote certain things and who didn't promote other things. Like George Clinton, like Funkadelic. What if Funkadelic was treated seriously as a rock band? It was psychedelic as could be. The entire landscape would be different if George Clinton was lionized the way Brian Wilson was lionized, the landscape would be different.

JH: And that was the role that folks like Jann Wenner played.

VR: Indeed. Don't forget Pete Cosey, by the way! My absolute. He was so off the grid and just so unusual that he couldn't fit in. Part of the reason why Cosey was so off the grid was because of the very things we're talking about— who got written about, who got respect. You know, at one point Pete Cosey could have very easily been seized upon. He was completely in that conversation in Chicago. But Pete Cosey got resistance from blue bloods. He incensed people.

But also, apparently, did John Lee Hooker. John Lee Hooker told Cosey, you need to get a haircut. You need to get a haircut and take that wah wah pedal and throw it in the lake. That's the other part of it is that the older generations, I mean… Albert King was not a Hendrix fan. Albert King said, "I don't know what that boy is playing, but it's not the blues." I'm sure that this hurt Jimi Hendrix to know that Albert King was not a fan. It's not just the underlying thing of white supremacy. Right? It's the concept of divide and rule. Black people are divided, you know, by their literal skin color. Right? And as the generational situation, you know, when bebop came in, Louis Armstrong was incensed. He could be intolerant his damn self. Right? Threatened by the next ship that comes in.

JH: Did you meet Prince? And did he relate to you as a contemporary?

VR: Kind of. We were playing at a club in Minneapolis. He could be quite elusive. He was at the club and he brought an artist that he was going to produce, but I didn't know. And at the end of the gig people said, "Oh man, Prince was here." I was like, WHAT? He could have said hello, I was mad as hell! And what happened was we're packing up and this big guy came and said, "Yo, the boss wanted me to tell you that the show was really good." He sent one of his bodyguards to let to let me know he enjoyed the show. I hold on to that.

JH: Any final thoughts about Prince?

VR: We can be preoccupied with the mechanics—humbled by the mechanics of the human body. So, to see Prince do what he did… it's humbling. Prince was able to utilize all the tools at his disposal, and all at once. His sense of melody, harmony, rhythm, stage presence, songcraft, parts, vocal tone, guitar tone was off the charts. In an almost superhuman way he was able to connect those things and then create a verisimilitude of life, a simulacrum of life. You know, deliver aspects of the human comedy. Take "Little Red Corvette." It's Prince's take on the classic rock 'n' roll car song. There was so much resistance to the idea of Black people playing rock 'n' roll music, and that song took on a very American trope, an obsession, car culture, the land of Springsteen and Rocket 88s. And it made us laugh and dance. It's about a car, but it's about more than a car, it's about a woman, and lots more. He plays kind of a composed, George Harrison-type solo on it, it sings, and then he wails. The rhythm part is a perfect rock guitar part. Prince blazed like a meteor—every note he played on the guitar was full of the spark of life.

Jerry Garcia

Dark Star

Live Dead (Warner Bros. 1969)

There are many Grateful Deads—the cosmic clowns, the psychedelic voyagers, the country band, the dance band, the jam band, the brilliant and moving, the lame and aggravating. They sum up the great dream of the 1960s, the voyage towards enlightenment, peace, love, and high times. Some of their compositions were brilliant, some of their performances were not. They could reach ecstatic peaks in wonderfully interactive improvisations, and yet sing out of tune, have wildly fluctuating tempos, indulge in meandering solos and miasmic one chord jams. They began as a social experiment, an idea born during the acid tests at Ken Kesey's ranch in 1965. It turns out that experiment not only survives the death of the band, it's growing. It's said that there are something like five thousand cover bands in the U.S. alone. The best of those cover bands, JRAD, attracts as big a crowd as the original band did in the 1970s when I attended most of my Dead shows.

All of the band members were smart and curious, but Jerry Garcia was the leader of the tribe. He had charisma, piercing intelligence, and wit. In the collection of folkies and soon-to-be rockers who circled their wagons in the Bay Area a few years before the Summer of Love he always seemed to have the most going on. Along with lyricist Robert Hunter he created as deep a songbook as any composer of the late 20th century.

Just as there are many Grateful Deads, there are many Jerry Garcias. There's the acoustic musician with deep knowledge of American roots, bluegrass, old time, ragtime, and country blues. There's the electric lead player with a devotion to melody and singing tone, the fuzzed-out rock and roller founded on Chuck Berry, the chiming country picker steeped in the Bakersfield sound, the mystic, the soul singer, the misfit, and the junkie. But perhaps the most provocative of his gifts was his exploratory side, touching on the avant-garde of the time, excursions that worked between keys, using feedback, bursts of notes, and effects to conjure other realms. There is no greater demonstration of this than the epic jams on the signature Dead song "Dark Star." Incredibly this song was proffered to Warner Brothers as a *studio single* in 1967! My how times have changed. "Dark Star" hasn't got a lot in common with Taylor Swift.

"Dark Star" was born of Ken Kesey's tests. We're still far from understanding the ripple effect of LSD not only on the arts of that era but on our entire culture. "Dark Star" is one of the flagship tripping tracks, all about the inner voyage, collective vectoring, and it was something brand new in electric music. Garcia never considered himself a jazz player, in fact he was rather dismissive of modern jazz, but his approach to "Dark Star" is suffused with the modal jazz explorations of the time. In "Dark Star" it's not just the notes that matter, it's the tone, the texture, the focus on group improvisation that makes it sing. I'm not sure it's even a song—more an experience. Jerry Garcia once said, "'Dark Star' has meant, while I'm playing it, almost as many things as I can sit here and imagine." (Jeff Tamarkin from an article in American Songwriter.)

The idea that rock musicians could get up there and free improvise for a half hour was pretty radical at the time. And yet obvious. It was an idea waiting to be born. Hendrix, Electric Flag, Cream, the Dead, they all were of a piece. This foundation in chance insured that a Dead concert would be an adventure. It was Esalen, the human consciousness movement, the adventures of The Merry Pranksters put into notes. The emphasis was on finding a group mind, all the parts equal, nothing off limits. Jazz players such as Ornette Coleman, Coltrane, Miles, Paul Bley, and Roscoe Mitchell had already been there, but the effect was entirely different in the hands of the Dead. None of them had near the vocabulary of their jazz counterparts, and this was part of the charm. The band developed their own language, like twins do, like a family that lives far from civilization. A subtext developed beyond the music, a search for unity out of chaos, all part of the zeitgeist of the times. Come together, find a meeting place, probe the unknown.

Sometimes the experiment failed. Sometimes these group improvisations, on "Dark Star" or other exploratory tunes, added up to nothing more than a bunch of noodling. Their audience was willing to allow failure in pursuit of the sublime. Sometimes I would listen to the Grateful Dead live and it would feel like a party with the guy who won't stop talking. A guy with sour breath who would get up close to me and blab in my face for 20 minutes about himself, exhausting my patience and goodwill. But to the Deadhead, mediocrity, if it eventually led to magic, was acceptable. This puzzlement, that you could play poorly in pursuit

Jerry Garcia (1977)

of transcendence, and still have hundreds of thousands of devotees, was something new in American music-making.

I asked Oteil Burbridge, bassist for Dead and Company, about all this. Oteil is a player of uncommon ability—in the parlance he has "chops." What was his perspective on this legacy of uneven performances? He told me that the band was all too aware of its limitations. They knew what great musicianship was, after all Bob Weir's first side project included Billy Cobham and Alphonse Mouzon in the rhythm section. But what they were after was something that had to withstand failure. It was bigger than any single member, bigger than any bad night. It was a democratic ideal whose success required the best and worst in each of them. When it worked, all the perdition was worth the wait.

Extrapolate upon this notion that "anything goes," and you have the curious matter of the legions of cover bands. Many are of modest ability. It leads you to wonder… perhaps execution, refinement, and accuracy may not be the point. This mindset is all but impossible to embrace for a jazz musician. But it's humanizing. When old hippies hear Dead music, whoever is playing it, they're not there for the musician's chops. They just want the song, the sensation, they get teary eyed, it's as if they're attending a religious service. I've played this music to a tough, toothless old postman with high blood pressure, a couple of stents, and a bad limp, and seen him melt into a little love puddle. In this sense the Dead might be called a gospel group, if the liturgy is a Dylanesque double entendre and the communion cup an artisanal IPA.

It's easy to turn up your nose at all of this. Many is the time I've heard musicians, especially in jazz, put a stink on the Dead. I'm sympathetic to their point of view. I stopped attending Grateful Dead shows in the '80s during the height of Garcia's heroin addiction because I was tired of watching them suck when I *knew* they could play well. But maybe people just need an excuse to gather and sing the hymn book of the '60s, and the devil be damned if it's out of key. Or to put it another way, if tens of thousands of people are getting their happy fix from 4,897 mediocre bands, and joy is the end result, along with billions of dollars of beer sales, it feels immoral to be snooty.

When the experiment works, there is a feeling in the room unlike any I have ever experienced in music. Something like a rocket ship taking off. It is a feeling of triumph, of tingling harmony, where everyone and everything is unified into a glowing ball of positive energy.

The recorded version of "Dark Star" from *Live Dead* is a good one, even if we miss the myriad surprises that occurred in every other live performance. Garcia leads the way but without imposing direction on the music, rather he suggests it. We have to acknowledge Bob Weir's rhythm playing in all this, too. Weir developed his own style of playing rhythm guitar, a language entirely built upon playing with the Grateful Dead from the age of 16 on. Much credit is due to him for his supportive work behind Garcia. The band's interplay, the disorienting effect of their light show, the ambient, ethereal sounds, the assortment of drums and bells in the rhythm section, the cowboy mysticism, made you feel as if you'd left the planet. It made small the tribulations of the world. Out of these weird musings the Dead would always play a rousing rock and roll tune that got all the hippies boogieing. Once at the fabled venue The Winterland the song they played after one of these long, psychedelic jams was "The Wheel," an anthemic tune with a cosmic Buddhist lyric and a celebratory progression and beat. The music exploded from the stage, and a huge ball started turning from the ceiling, bullets of light showering down on the audience. Everybody began to roar, and the band kicked into a higher gear. The crowd roared more, and there was a jolt of electricity that went through the whole hall, connecting us all.

A moment like this can hook you for life.

Garcia's life itself towards the end was no model for living. Given the chemicals he put into his body it's a miracle he lived as long as he did. It's further proof of an astonishing truth. He, and the band, did pretty much everything wrong and it all worked out right. This success story is unlike any other that I know of—anywhere. It all started out with such radiant beginnings. Everything was possible. It's sad to think of all the songs he and Hunter never wrote due to Jerry's habit. For years, this most public man isolated himself in a stupor in a small, dark apartment in Marin County. Fortunately, he had something of a comeback and returned to form for a few years before he left us.

Never mind his demise, though—Jerry's life story is one of celebration. It's about the *connection* the listeners took away. Anyone who loves music has felt it, whether from Stevie Wonder, or John Coltrane, or the trance music of Morocco. Chasing that connection, in its many venues and manifestations, has kept the instrument in my hands all these years. Often I've wanted to concede to my own shortcomings, to the humiliations and depredations of the music industry. But I can't. Met, even once, by this transcendent magic in music, the questing soul can't turn away.

John Abercrombie

Ghost Dance

Characters (ECM 1978)

John Abercrombie was one of the most important guitarists of his generation. Why do I lead with that? Because I think he's one of those musicians people will too easily forget. He was among the first artists to record for the fledgling ECM label in the early 1970s—when people talk about the "ECM sound" they are partly referring to John's breakout records. There's a folk element to the jazz, poly chords over open grooves, space, cinematic drama. Some of it is *burning*, technique to die for. Other times the sound is dreamier, shifting moods and tempos, the guitar more texture than notes.

The track "Ghost Dance" is an outlier in the Abercrombie opus. It's from his only solo record, *Characters*. It's ambient, ethereal, a series of overdubs using open tunings on acoustic, harmonics, a soprano guitar, overdriven electric, and even mandolin. You almost feel it lacks direction until he zaps you with a clear, pointed melody and a chord change. The rhythm comes just from the guitars, and there's dance in it that echoes the title. With those ECM reverbs, the overall effect is heavenly. You forget it's guitars you're hearing, there's a mystery to the track, you feel dropped into a shadowy ritual. When people make music like this now, with looping pedals and digital technology, it's a more obvious choice.

But to hear a kick-ass jazz player do this back then, someone who could play any bebop tune at any tempo, this was different. It's almost all texture, which in and of itself was somewhat new. His reticence makes the track whole, the dialogue created between John and John, all those different strings vibrating at different rates, mysterious bleeps and blops, long-held drones. Close your eyes and leave the earth.

The Ghost Dance was a Plains Indian ritual from the latter part of the 1800s designed to bring the spirit world alive to drive away the white colonialists who had destroyed Native American lives and culture. As word of the ritual spread, this sacred dance was embraced by thousands of Indians, and a leader named Wowovka, who was said to have brought the dance from the spirit world, traveled from tribe to tribe as a prophet. Imagine these people dancing on the Plains, praying for healing, for renewal, for survival. A beautiful, heart-wrenching sight. We know what came next—Wounded Knee.

"Ghost Dance"—a bold title indeed.

John Abercrombie with Jack De Johnette
Red Creek, Rochester, N.Y. (1976)

John, also known as "Crumbles," and Larry Coryell were amongst the first jazz players to step on a fuzzbox in the late '60s, and early on John had blazing chops. In the early '70s he did several high-profile gigs with fusioneers such as the Brecker Brothers and Billy Cobham. But that sound didn't suit him. He eventually abandoned the guitar pick, preferring the sound of the thumb, and gradually moved towards more introspective lyricism, with his own simple but not simple tunes. On *Timeless*, his first ECM record, he tore up the fretboard. That record sold very well, and up until the end of his life fans would bring that LP to him to sign after a show. It bugged him. "What about all the other stuff I've done!"

John did duos with Ralph Towner and Scofield, and he did a big band session with Bob Brookmeyer. In the 1970s he was the go-to for everyone. But all he really wanted was to write his own music and play with the people who mattered to him. He stayed with the same producer, Manfred Eicher of ECM, his whole career. Others around him may have been cultivating a variety of bands and projects, but John focused on

John Abercrombie © Roberto Masotti / ECM Records

his quartet music, the tunes with odd numbers of bars, some Bartok harmony, poignant melodies, and short forms.

One of his late-life band members told me this story from around 2014—he received a phone call from John as he was sound-checking for a gig.

"Hey, where are you, whaddya doing?" John asked.

"At the Jazz Standard getting ready to play, what's up with you?"

"I'm at home ... everybody's out playing, I got no work. I have like two gigs next month."

What could his bandmate say?

There's no pension in jazz. No safety net.

Abercrombie smoked, drank, and ate what he wanted, he enjoyed his life, played his own music, did what he loved, and never was one to hustle for favor or play any games.

Sonic Youth

Brave Men Run (In My Family)

(Homestead Records 1985)

by Nels Cline

I've known Nels Cline my entire adult life and he has always been a source of knowledge and inspiration. We've had many a discussion about our jazz, classic rock, and avant-garde heroes—but unlike me, Nels has a formative background in (what is now called) indie rock. Who were his biggest influences, I wondered? Sonic Youth is a band I never listened to. But after reading this essay I not only understand Nels better—I listen to Sonic Youth!

In 1984 I was 28 years old and had been working for several years at the famous Rhino Records store in my home zone of West Los Angeles, California. I was also playing in various projects of what one might term jazz or experimental music on both acoustic and electric guitars, including Quartet Music (acoustic), Rhythm Plague (electric), Julius Arthur Hemphill & the J.A.H. Band (electric), Charlie Haden's Liberation Music Orchestra West Coast (acoustic), and Wayne Peet's Doppler Funk (electric).

As a record store geek and a guitar geek, I had explored guitar and guitar-centric music with considerable interest verging on obsession since

I was in my early teens. My point in mentioning this is to explain that, being an ardent fan of both "legit" types of guitar (blues, straight-ahead jazz, classical guitar, various folk/fingerstyle forms) and "experimental" guitar music from around that time (Fred Frith, Derek Bailey, Keith Rowe, Hans Reichl, Eugene Chadbourne) along with my past and present growth out of rock 'n' roll (from psychedelic to blues-infused to prog to punk/no wave lacerations) hearing oddly episodic compositional forms and odd, original tunings and microtonality was pretty normal for me. Taking this all into account, I often marvel at the impact that hearing early Sonic Youth recordings had on me—a lasting impact, to say the least. It seems that I can't avoid tossing chunks of autobiographical material into this, my humble attempt to explain something that can be difficult to explain. Why *do* we respond to sounds, to *art*? What are we thinking? Or are we mostly *feeling*? I am leaning towards the latter as my overall assessment.

Working in Glenn Branca's large and loud guitar orchestras in his seminal "Symphonies," the twin towers of Sonic Youth, Thurston Moore and Lee Ranaldo, had a real leg up on open-tuned guitar resonances/sonorities. It was apparently during this time that Thurston and Lee gravitated to each other and, along with bassist Kim Gordon, got the Sonic Youth ball rolling. I heard Sonic Youth's first record, an EP called *Sonic Youth* (on Glenn Branca's Neutral label) when it was new—around 1981. I was working as the warehouse manager of an import record distributor in Long Beach California, and for some reason this importer carried three American independent labels: Twin Tone, ROIR cassettes, and Neutral. My reaction to the Neutral EP was ... pretty neutral, actually. As someone preoccupied with music coming out of New York, I guess I expected a little more bluster, shrapnel, twisted something-or-other. Ah, expectations ...

I worked at Rhino Records with a truly remarkable team of employees, one of whom was the writer and eventual independent record label maverick Byron Coley. One day Byron played the first Sonic Youth full-length album, *Confusion Is Sex* in the store. Now I was intrigued! I was particularly grabbed by the songs "Shaking Hell" and "She's In A Bad Mood." This led me to Sonic Youth's "Zensor EP" (on the import Zensor label, hence that appellation), which contained the truly jarring

"Brother James" and poetic "Early American." This music was at once extremely raw and poetic, brash while also being able to summon a mysterious, haunted quality. It also struck me as kind of sexy in an angst-y way. (Angst was a frequent element in rock music in this general period, of course.)

One of the many denizens of the record store was a young man named Mike Sheppard who had a label called Iridescence. As the indie and import rock buyer at the time, I was frequently buying records from and chatting with these young and often rather eccentric entrepreneurs—besides Mike, people like Calvin Johnson, Mike Muir, and so many others. Mike Sheppard had a big personality and was often barefoot. He was truly passionate, even ambitious and yeah, he could be kind of obnoxious, but he was releasing interesting albums with really cool graphic-designed covers from bands and musicians like Jad Fair with Half Japanese, Gary Kail/Zurich 1916, Twisted Roots, Eugene Chadbourne, and more.

One day Mike came in with this new 7" by Sonic Youth, "Death Valley '69" featuring Lydia Lunch with a B-side of "Brave Men Run (In My Family)." At this time I had little interest in Lydia Lunch's whole vibe (ironic, because years later I toured and recorded a bit with her and I love her), so I turned my attention to the B-side, "Brave Men Run." This song has a strong, near-heroic opening, instrumental for the whole first half, and the de-tuned CLANG of the track got me right away. It still does—more so than the later version on their *Bad Moon Rising* album (which is great, of course, but different). It's the *sound*, I think. This was before Sonic Youth used any effects pedals, distortion, etc. Cheap, open-tuned guitars, plus bass and drums in a glorious kind of twanged-out symphony. Epic without being like the bloated prog I often swooned over in high school.

Around this same time someone told me that Thurston Moore from Sonic Youth wanted his band to be able to play more gigs at more venues in Los Angeles and that he was going to call me to get any suggestions I might have. What?! I couldn't even play gigs in Los Angeles unless my bandmates booked them ourselves! We were pretty hopeless and not really "on the scene," being kind of uncool, nerdy jazz fusion types.

Since being asked to write about this moment, and the effect that this song and Sonic Youth have had on me generally, I will try to explain. But now we are treading on very subjective, personal, ephemeral turf. Here's all I know— the combination of my *feeling* upon hearing this music plus some sense of identification with what I perceived of as a wondrous, intuitive group creativity and dynamic was and still is food for my soul. As I followed Sonic Youth in the many years after this recording, and ultimately ended up being friendly with them and even collaborating with most of them, I always felt a kind of shudder or tingle upon hearing not just the sounds, but upon experiencing the decisions that they made—or my perception of their decision-making, anyway. Certain songs exhibit great patience in terms of tension and release ("Shoot," Trilogy"), others are like bursts of pure cauterizing white light ("Catholic Block," "Drunken Butterfly").

"Brave Men Run" is formally almost structurally the opposite of certain songs that emerged not long after this 7"—songs like "Tuff Gnarl" and "Schizophrenia," with thrilling instrumental codas. "Brave Men Run" starts with an exhilarating instrumental theme before kind of airing out as Kim Gordon moans her rather oblique lyrics. (The fact that this title came from an Ed Ruscha painting already steeped in Ruscha's wordplay and sly references only adds to my fascination.) It's a convergence of sounds and signals, of sexiness and intelligence and nerdiness that sounds *great* to me. And on top of all that, I love bands. I'm a "band guy." (That should be obvious by now.)

So strong was my identification with Sonic Youth after hearing "Brave Men Run" and beyond that I became quite the foaming fanboy. I made statements like, "After hearing Sonic Youth I wish I could un-learn everything I've been trying to learn all this time," and "Listening to Sonic Youth is like having someone stroke my DNA." (Yeah, I actually said that more than once!) Pretty silly, you say. Maybe. But my exposure to and love of Sonic Youth's music and what I perceived as their intuitive methodologies *did* alter the course of my music-making as I deigned to add the overtones to my palette that I heard achieved and truly honored in their music. I also found their pounding, droning, more ritualistic moments quite intoxicating. What *were* those incredible textures and resonant sonorities, those non-specifically pitched, exhilarating noises??

Besides all that could be said about Lee and Thurston's myriad tunings—and there are a *lot* of those, most of which I don't know—a crucial ingredient is the length of strings behind the bridge, which can be played to shimmering/shattering effect, bent with a tremolo arm, scraped. I needed to acquire a guitar that had these properties, and in the heaps of cheap and nearly-broken guitars that went into creating a Sonic Youth song or show, the Fender Jazzmaster and Jaguar—often with knobs and pickups altered or ripped out—stood out. I didn't really know the difference between the two instruments other than their pickups, but those guitars were really inexpensive in the '80s, so I picked up a 1966 Jaguar, the first guitar of the two models to appear in the *Recycler* after I returned from a tour with Julius Hemphill. So comfortable to play! And strings behind the bridge! To think that I and practically everyone I knew growing up derided these guitars! I was off to the races!

The various ways one can utilize these strings could be a lengthy diatribe, so I will spare you. Let's just say that at this point there is no way for me to overstate the significance of these sounds to me. And I eventually moved to using a Jazzmaster as my main guitar, mainly because of the pickups' sound and the extra string length, and accompanying extra

Sonic Youth (1987)

string tension. I started a personal campaign of playing slight out-of-tune unison notes whenever possible to excite the overtone potential of certain parts. I do this with Wilco, on various recordings by singer/songwriters, composer/improvisers—not just in my own stuff. I had already explored open tunings in a Ralph Towner, John Fahey, Alex DeGrassi kind of way, but now I had new ideas along such lines. Amidst the indie glam and art smart posturing one may associate with Sonic Youth, there exists, central to everything, one essential—the *sound*—often to ecstatic effect, at least to the ears of this jazz/fusion/prog/punk polymath. And it's not like I am alone in being inspired by this music, as potent de-tuned and open-tuned progenitors such as Polvo, Unwound, Dust Devils, early Blonde Redhead, and many, many more did their unique deep dives into the Sonic whirlpool. Sometimes one feels so transported by sound that it seems that one's being is being simultaneously eradicated and amplified. It's quite a *feeling*, and one that is intensely pleasurable to seek out, to return to, to cherish.

Flash forward a few years and I found myself asked to play on a Rickie Lee Jones record, the seriously excellent *The Evening Of My Best Day*. It seems that Rickie Lee just loves Mike Watt's album *Contemplating The Engine Room*, his first opera and to my mind, a brilliantly conceived work. So, there I was along with Watt and Stephen Hodges—the crew from that record—about to try tracking this song with Rickie Lee Jones singing and playing acoustic guitar, and my first idea was to try using my very neo-Thurston open-tuned Hagstrom guitar. After initial probing, a take or two, the voice of this lovely guitarist/co-producer named David sounded in my headphones, telling me that my guitar was out of tune. "That's intentional," I told him and everyone there. Big silence. "Okay, I'll switch guitars!" I'm not sure there's a lesson to be learned here, save for that sometimes the wondrous, wobbling CLANG of the Sonic universe needs its own space and time to invite the ecstatic. But in that space and in that time is where I love to reside whenever possible.

Songs from my records wherein one can hear the influence of Sonic Youth: Thurston County, The Rite (for Ingrid Thulin), Progression, Blood Drawing, He Still Carries A Torch For Her, Cymbidium, Lapsing (part 2), Sister Hotel.

Ritchie Blackmore

Speed King

Deep Purple In Rock (Warner Bros. 1970)

"When I was 20, I didn't give a damn about song construction. I just wanted to make as much noise and play as fast and as loud as possible."
—Ritchie Blackmore, *Guitar World* interview

Now *this* is a guitar player talking. Blackmore, along with Allan Holdsworth, are the two non-Americans in this book. Why? Because his playing is so central to where the electric guitar ended up in rock 'n' roll in America. These days everyone talks about the influence of Jeff Beck and Jimny Page—but as a player (not a composer) Blackmore influenced *them*.

And what could be more American than this fabulously stupid and wonderful quote. Blackmore and Deep Purple epitomize everything over the top about 1970's rock music. They leave behind the intellect Zeppelin cultivated and go straight to the crotch. With incredible accuracy and passion, and all the chops anyone could ever wish for, these guys made rock 'n' roll the sonic equivalent of a Pontiac Trans Am. Deep Purple spawned legions of imitators and satirists.

Watching the footage of Ritchie and the gang live from that era makes me want to pop a few frosties and take the car out for a 100 mile per hour spin. It makes me want my hair back.

It's instructive to mark the enormous change in Deep Purple between 1968 and 1970. Only two years before the record *Deep Purple In Rock* they sounded like a more freaky, rocked out version of the Zombies, sporting Beatle-like bowl haircuts, frilled shirts, and proper jackets. Before that, Blackmore played in a teenybopper outfit circa 1964 called the Outlaws who dressed in matching cream-colored duds and shook their booties in choreography that would have fit right into American Bandstand. Somehow this guy transformed himself from a square into one of the most outrageous performers in modern history. And I'm not sure he actually believed the line I started this piece with. There's substance to some of Purple's writing.

Zeppelin changed Deep Purple. They decided to get "heavier," brought in a new howler for a singer, Ian Gillen, and started to go for the jugular. They competed with Black Sabbath for primacy. These were the times in England, the Beatles were out, and ear-splitting, grandiose androgyny was in.

Never mind their anthem "Smoke on the Water," as perfect and parodied a guitar hook as ever existed. "Speed King" is an episodic piece with utterly inane lyrics, god-bless-them "jazzy" organ and guitar modal interplay, a gangbusters guitar solo, and a trademark thunderous climax that makes me want to yell, "FUCK YEAH!" Jon Lord's classical training is in evidence on the Hammond organ and Blackmore plays with a kind of crushing intensity that was new for the time. It wasn't quite as bluesy or subtle as Jimmy Page or Clapton, as R&B/ freakazoid as Jimi, or as artful as Jeff Beck. It was a primal scream. No one had technique like Blackmore, and save for Jimi Hendrix, no one had coaxed more unearthly sounds from the instrument—shuddering wails, sobs, squonks, and scratches.

He was lionized not so much by his contemporaries, like Page and Jeff Beck (athough they were in awe of his chops) but by his successors, Steve Vai, Vivian Campbell. What we see in Blackmore is the genesis of heavy metal— circus-like theatrics, styled hair, make up, and leather pants were just around the corner. Blackmore still sounds relatively free of the pitiable artifice and pretension that ensued. He *yowls* with just a few notes. The music still contains a childish glee that seems quite cheery compared to, say, Judas Priest or Marilyn Manson.

I must also mention Blackmore's solo on "Highway Star," on Deep Purple's subsequent album *Machine Head*. This anthemic burner was supposedly written in just a few minutes, and like "Speed King," has lyrics that spoke directly to 16-year-old boys for whom a driver's license

Ritchie Blackmore, Hamburg, Germany (1971)

and puberty were still a novelty. Groups like Yes and King Crimson had begun to assimilate European classical music into their writing, and here Blackmore and Lord show off some Baroque chops to delightful, heroic effect. Unlike those other bands, though, with Deep Purple the focus is not on compositional sophistication. It's designed not for pondering or reflection, but for fucking and getting a speeding ticket.

Let us pause to celebrate all the great pop songs about cars: "Rocket 88," "Maybelline," "Little Red Corvette," "Racing in the Street," "Born to Be Wild," "Low Rider." And, of course, the "car as woman" metaphor is one of rock's most obvious and tired tropes.

I read that Deep Purple was named the loudest band in the world after a 1972 Wembley Stadium concert. That's nothing to be proud of. It's just plain dumb. But kind of cool. You can't imagine how loud four Marshall stacks are up close, nor can I. Just one Marshall stack is bone-rattling. How is Blackmore not completely deaf? By the seventies, PA systems had finally developed to the point where a concert in a stadium could sound OK. More's the pity for the music. Stadiums were the death knell of subtlety and intimacy.

I get delicious and guilty pleasure from this phase of guitar history.

Ralph Towner

Nimbus

Solstice (ECM Records 1975)

In the right hands the guitar is a small orchestra. Joe Pass can play a standard, any standard, and it's a fully formed entity. Bass, accompaniment, groove, melody—it's all there. Such is the case with much of Ralph Towner's output.

Ralph, alas, has somewhat lost currency amongst a younger generation, though he's one of our greatest composers, stylists, and improvisers. He began as a jazz pianist and classical horn player, but in 1962 at age 22 had a eureka moment, deciding to learn classical guitar. He practiced obsessively, and thereafter formed the seminal group, Oregon. This band was one of the finest, most original ensembles of this era. They found a way to bring oboe, English horn, tabla, sitar, guitar, and bass into one dynamic, ever-evolving organism. Ralph, to me, is foremost a composer. He plays like a composer whether in duos with vibraphonist Gary Burton, orchestral arrangements with Oregon, fully notated works for classical guitar, or free improvs. All are exploratory and yet touch the soul. Writers struggle when trying to label this music. That's one way we know it's special.

Ralph had already made a big impact by 1975 when Nimbus was

released. Oregon had released five records and he'd appeared on Weather's Report's 1972 album *I Sing the Body Electric* on 12-string. On one astonishing track, "The Moors," Ralph played an acoustic introduction, a rather surprising addition to one of the seminal *electric* fusion bands. It's harmonically ambitious, wild, and even kind of funky. Ralph told me that what's on the recording is him warming up, he didn't know the mics were on. When he said he was ready to record, bandleader Joe Zawinul said, "No, you're done!" It was the first time anyone had played 12-string guitar in this kind of modern jazz setting. The acoustic 12-string guitar is a bitch to play. It eats up your fingernails, its neck is wide and unwieldy, it's awfully hard to tune. Leadbelly used one mid-century, Leo Kottke set a new and impossibly high bar in the '70s. But no one played it like Ralph.

Ralph Towner with Oregon at Bach Dancing & Dynamite Society, Half Moon Bay CA (1989)

The Norwegian Quartet from 1975, with Jan Garbarek, Jon Christenson, and Eberhard Weber, was doing something new, and Ralph's spectacular writing brought out the best in them. The composition of "Nimbus," on which he played the 12-string, is fairly simple. A two-bar melody in 12/8 time modulates over a 12- bar form. It might as well be a blues tune. What makes it so impactful is the *huge* sound of the 12-string, the unique tuning, and Ralph's dramatic picking and strumming patterns which are as percussive as they are melodic. He's practically playing the thing like a drum. I love his comping on this track, a talent he honed partly by being a pianist.

Alternate tunings had been used before, Charlie Patton and Son House tuned to open G and D, Joni Mitchell, Robbie Basho, Alex DeGrassi, and John Fahey based their sound around them. But no one had ever heard a tuning, or a sound on the guitar like this. The guitar rings and chimes and all the overtones become like a carillon. The quartet has intense drama, the groove feels organic, there's nothing manufactured, it feels fresh, alive, percolating with energy. Garbarek's solo is incantatory, brawny, Christensen is both open and grooving, and Weber 's mournful melisma leaves you feeling like you just broke up with someone.

In my interview with Ralph in my 2021 book *Guitar Talk* he says that one of his strategies for composing with this group was to write out chords with no fixed bar lines. He'd cue the chord change when it was time. Although this tune seems like it's within a form, you feel that open spontaneity, they're building, and building some more, and at just the right moment breaking out to another strata.

1975 was in incredible year in music. *Koln Concert*, *The Hissing of Summer Lawns*, *Blow by Blow*, *Blood on the Tracks*, *Wish You Were Here*, *Bob Marley and The Wailers Live*. In the midst of it all, Ralph was making a relatively quiet but lasting statement. The term "chamber jazz" had recently been coined. Other bands were incorporating sounds from around the world—but none sounded remotely like Oregon. The acoustic guitar, Bach, gamelan, West African kora, Indian music, and Bill Evans all dining at the same table. This music wasn't founded on the blues or bebop (although these musicians knew that lineage.) It was improvised music with its own signature, reference points, and goals.

Today the jazz scene, especially in Europe, is overflowing with every hybrid under the sun. Ralph saw it coming.

I saw Oregon in 1976 at Royce Hall in L.A. with my new friend, Nels Cline. It was hugely impactful. One of the things that struck me was their free improvising, which I learned they did at every show—amazing chemistry, the way they listened to each other, reaching bracing spaces—and so *quiet* in contrast to the growing din in the world of electric music. We hung around and watched them pack up, making small talk, groupies of a kind. If memory serves the whole band fit in ONE station wagon that they backed up to the stage entrance. It had wood paneling as I recall. Surely, I thought, musicians of this caliber had a bus, or were whisked away by limousine to the airport. They were driving all night to the next gig—Portland maybe? My education was just beginning.

Ralph Towner and the author. Photo by Scott Friedlander.

Cornell Dupree

Bridge Over Troubled Water–Aretha Franklin

Live at Fillmore West (Atlantic 1971)

by Adam Levy

Adam Levy has focus as a guitarist—a minimalist's touch and an attention to time and feel.

In asking him to contribute I hoped he would choose a player who also valued these same attributes. Indeed he did. Dupree was one of a number of rhythm guitarists who shaped the sound of my childhood. The R&B music of the late '60s and early '70s was hugely influential, not just to me but to the whole world. As I've said elsewhere, the folks who played this music were often invisible, they were there to support the stars, the singers. Dupree performed with the best. I'm thrilled that Adam wrote about this subtle, deep, and important musician and a track that brings his virtuosity into focus.

When I was 20 years old, I was asked to join a 12-piece band led by Charlie Mead—a friend I'd met while studying at the Dick Grove School of Music in Los Angeles. The band played updated arrangements of classic R&B songs from the 1950s and '60s, and some original songs as well. Honestly, I may not have been the best man for the job, as my guitar

Cornell Dupree

style leaned more toward contemporary jazz at that time. I had heard the familiar Motown hits on the radio, and I owned one James Brown album, but I always thought of the guitars on these records as part of the whole sound. I'd never focused on learning any specific licks or parts.

Charlie, for whatever reason, had faith in me, and did what he could to help me learn R&B guitar. He often recommended songs and players for me to check out. Steve Cropper was one of his favorites—especially on the track "Hip Hug-Her" by Booker T. & the MG's. Charlie also got me listening to Mickey Baker, Bruce Conte (from Tower of Power), and Cornell Dupree.

Oh, man. *Cornell Dupree.*

This was the mid-1980s—many years before internet search engines. It was harder to trace players' discographies then, let alone get the actual records. I dug through the crates of my favorite used-record shops and bought every album with Dupree that I could find. Charlie was right! He sounded incredible on everything I heard—with King Curtis, with Stuff, with Donny Hathaway.

During this Dupree deep-dive period, one LP that I just couldn't get enough of was Aretha Franklin's *Live at Fillmore West*. The album features the choicest cuts recorded over three consecutive March nights in 1971. Franklin is backed by tenor saxophonist King Curtis and his incomparable band, which included (along with Dupree) bassist Jerry Jemmott, drummer Bernard Purdie, and Hammond organist Billy Preston.

The album opens with a blazing version of "Respect"—one of Franklin's signature numbers. If anyone else tried singing and playing the song at this pace, it might feel uncomfortably frenetic, but she and the band take the ride with grace and prowess. A funkified "Love the One You're With" comes up next. The song was a hit for singer-songwriter Stephen Stills (of Crosby, Stills & Nash) at the time of Franklin's performance. The Queen of Soul makes it her own.

The album's third track is "Bridge Over Troubled Water"—a 1970 chart-topper for Simon & Garfunkel. Franklin sets the mood with an instrumental verse up front—playing the vocal melody on electric piano while the band simmers. Dupree lightly plays chords on the backbeats, complementing drummer Purdie's deep pocket. Nothing fancy, really, but it's absolutely perfect.

Thirty seconds in, as the song gets to the pre-chorus, Dupree turns up the heat—climbing the fretboard chromatically, harmonizing a melody in parallel 6ths. It's a move he has played before and since, but it has never sounded more consummately placed than this. He finishes out this section with more backbeat chords and subtle fills.

Purdie breaks from his staid pattern at 1:23, making room for the backing vocalists to croon, *"Don't trouble the water…"* Franklin finally joins in singing as well. Here, Dupree sneaks in tasteful bends and volume-knob swells between the vocal lines, building on their energy without ever crowding them. This eight-measure section is a masterclass on how guitarists can play with singers: *Don't get in the way, but don't be shy. Play something that makes the music better—or play nothing at all.*

Dupree returns to backbeat *chanks* for the next verse, fills with more 6ths throughout the pre-chorus and chorus that follow, and returns to bending and swelling for the post-chorus breakdown—leaning into his notes a little harder this time.

Franklin takes one more lap around the song form, singing *so* powerfully. As the band and backing vocalists elevate to meet her, Dupree returns to the same strategies he has plied throughout the song, yet there's no sense of copy-and-paste. Every phrase feels fresh and in synch with the moment.

Dupree's tone on this track—and throughout the album—is more stringy and clear than is usual for him. It sounds almost as if they put a microphone in front of his Telecaster and blended that with the amp sound, though it's *very* unlikely that that's the case. A more plausible explanation is the unusual amplifier that Dupree apparently used on this recording—an Acoustic 260 head and an Acoustic 261 cabinet with a horn. While I've never seen this amp mentioned in articles on Cornell Dupree (he's usually pegged as a Fender man, preferring Twin Reverb amps), there is some grainy footage of the Fillmore West performances on YouTube and this Acoustic rig seems to be the behemoth behind him. Using a powerful solid-state amp and a speaker cab with a horn certainly would render a clean, detailed sound.

The thing that's true of *all* the greatest players is, of course, true with regard to Dupree—whatever equipment he happened to use here, he was going to sound exactly like himself. Have a listen, play along if you can, and see for yourself just how personal and unique Cornell Dupree's musicianship was.

I could continue, talking about the rest of this soul-stirring album. But to be honest, I rarely get past "Bridge Over Troubled Water." It's just so great. If someday—God forbid—my doctor ever says to me, "I'm sorry, Mr. Levy. You've only got 5 minutes and 49 seconds left to live," I hope to spend that time listening to this track.

Cornell Dupree in Montreux, Switzerland (1976)

Joni Mitchell and Larry Carlton

Amelia

Hejira (Asylum 1976)

Of all the musicians to emerge from the California folk scene of the 1960s, save Jerry Garcia, Joni Mitchell was the most original guitar player. Sure, Stephen Stills played the heck out of a Les Paul, and Roger McGuinn's Rickenbacker 12-string became an anthemic touchstone. But Joni Mitchell's use of open tunings in her songs is an example of an artist completely re-purposing the guitar to meet her needs as a songwriter.

In the Ralph Towner chapter, I also discussed open tunings. Ralph's sound was oriented around the 12-string, and he was an improviser which Joni was not. Joni used open tunings on a six string to shape her compositions, and according to what I've read she used over 50 different tunings.

In a recent tribute to Joni at the Hollywood Bowl my friend Marvin Sewell was asked to occupy the guitar chair. He spoke to me of the enormous challenge of replicating all these tunings when he had no guitar tech and could only bring a couple of guitars. During rehearsals, he had to change keys for various singers. He had to retune over and over again. Finally, he was forced to mostly use standard tuning. Hearing this testimony makes you aware of just how central Mitchell's guitar sound was to her creations.

There are many reasons why the guitar is unique to the family of musical instruments. This is one of them. You can tune it any way you want. Fred Frith would often detune his guitar when free improvising. Jimi Hendrix tuned a half step down because he liked the feel of the guitar at that tension, and it made singing a little easier. French artist Mark Ducret sometimes detunes his guitar to achieve one-of-a-kind harmonies. Kurt Rosenwinkel did an entire record in an open tuning. Amazingly he improvises with complete fluency in the new tuning which is unbelievably challenging. None of the notes lie where you are used to seeing them when you retune.

I find the track "Amelia" extremely moving. The lyrics are stunning. But the guitar playing is a big part of what makes this song so bittersweet, so full of longing. She tunes to an open C in this piece, C,G,C,E,C,E. One of the things this tuning affords with certain fingerings is the bite of minor seconds against open strings. When you tune like this, it allows the guitar to resonate in a way that standard tuning does not. Without getting too much into the weeds, an open tuning allows more of the

Larry Carlton (1987)

Joni Mitchell (1983)

upper partial harmonics to ring. What's interesting here, also, is the odd time signature phrases she throws in, allowing the flow of the lyrics to dictate the guitar part. When she played this song live, she simplified the guitar part, and it's easy to see why. It's complicated, and I guess she didn't want to have to replicate all of the nuance on stage while singing.

Larry Carlton's support on this track is every bit as stunning as Mitchell's chords. At first you're sure it's a pedal steel guitar. It is not. Larry Carlton uses harmonics, a whammy bar, and subtle string pulls to emulate a pedal steel. The textures he brings, ghostly, ethereal, like a genie floating above the desert floor, do far more than simply accompany the track. They transform it. This is the great genius of a top tier studio player. Larry is able to find the soul of the song and build a part that exponentially advances that emotion.

I'll take this opportunity to further rave about Larry Carlton. Of course, there's his famous solo on Steely Dan's "Kid Charlemagne." Slightly less feted is "Third World Man" in which Carlton creates an instrumental hook that adds considerably to the arc of the song. You'd be hard pressed to find better guitar tone than this. His line is as singable as Donald Fagen's melody. But then Carlton worked this magic on hundreds of records. That ability to disappear into someone else's creation, to boost it, is a wonder. It takes a certain personality. You have to be a *giver*. I've always loved his work with The Crusaders—a tasty blend of jazz, rhythm and blues, and funk. He's one of the most emulated guitar players of our times.

When we think of great guitar players we often think of dexterity, of speed, of original chord voicings, or wild electronics. The playing by both these artists on this track goes against all that. It's quiet, subtle, haunting, and supremely original. Like all great guitar playing where vocals are involved, these two artists have one purpose—to support the song.

On her website Mitchell describes penning this song after breaking up with a lover. It was written in a series of motel rooms while travelling across the country. Many great Nashville songwriters sit in a room to write, they show up in the morning and keep office hours into the afternoon. You hear it in their work. I don't think you write a song like "Amelia" in an office.

It's gratifying to see Joni Mitchell finally get her due in 2023 with prestigious awards and prizes, giving acclaimed performances after decades of being out of the limelight. Her victory lap was not a given. For years she complained of not being adequately valued, and then she was disabled by a brain aneurysm. I don't think anyone was sure whether she would emerge from it whole. Thanks in part to Brandi Carlile she's now being honored in spectacular ways. Let's honor Larry, too.

Willie King

I Am the Blues

I Am the Blues (Self-release 2000)

I wrote the bulk of this piece in 2002 not long after my first journey south to the Delta. It was a vision quest of sorts. I'd just broken up with my first wife, and I was a bit lost. I visited Dockery Farms, Beale Street, B.B. King's birthplace in Indianola, a juke joint called Po Monkey's in Clarksdale, and Bettie's Place, the odyssey I've detailed below.

I considered writing about Charlie Patton for this book. He's at the root of all Delta blues, and one of *the* hubs of all American roots music. I felt his presence during my blues hejira. But I wondered what more could be said about one of the most haunting, impactful, and prodigious talents in guitar history. Many a researcher has weighed in. Did I have anything to add? Then it occurred to me I'd met someone who was a living link to that history, Willie King. To introduce Willie, I need a Patton prologue.

Patton was, as far as we know, the first "eclectic" guitar showman. He played hillbilly songs, deep blues, gospel, and nineteenth century parlor songs. Patton was mixed race, probably part Indian and Caucasian, and in that light we can see he was a prophecy, the blueprint for performers of all races who came after. It's said that his voice was so loud you could hear it 500 yards away. His singing style, which influenced Howlin' Wolf, has its aural roots in a type of African singing called voice chording. Though he played stages in New York and Chicago, his main gigs were close to his home of Dockery Plantation, now called Dockery Farms, in Mississippi. When I hear his recordings, whether a rag, moaning blues, or a story song, I try to picture the physical space. What was a Saturday night like at the Dockery Plantation in the early 1900s, where a one-man band brought brief respite to the sharecroppers in some shack far from the Big House? What was *that* party like? No bass and drums, no PA, just a wild-looking fellow in the corner wailing away on a steel guitar, singing as loud as he could as the folks drank, sweated, and danced, shedding the weight of the work week. My experience at Bettie's Place may have been as close as you can get to that scene in the 21st century.

Willie King, born in 1943, was part of that Delta blues lineage. He wasn't an innovator like Patton or Robert Johnson. But you hear the line going all the way back to West Africa, in the way he lays down a one-chord boogie, patient and urgent at the same time, his rough-edged voice making you hurt and smile at the same time.

The track I've chosen, "I Am the Blues" represents Willie's laid back and yet intense style. It's got a country blues feel, less hard-hitting than a Chicago shuffle, but every bit as deep. He's playing the tradition, reaching all the way back to the beginning of the 20th century. Sure, the band is electric, but they could be delivering the same groove, the same bite, with acoustic instruments. It's on a self-published record that is hard to find, but you can find the track on YouTube (youtu.be/ebH6xpjy99c).

Willie King turned his back on the touring life, and he hardly recorded at all. His calling was to show up at his neighborhood spot most weeks. This was his community, his fellow farmers. I'm indebted to his bassist, I'll call him TK, for inviting me to one of the most wondrous gigs I've ever done.

TK is driving northeast towards the Alabama border. The vents in his 1970 Toyota won't stop blowing hot air, so all the windows are open. A fan sits beside him, powered by the cigarette lighter. We're going to Bettie's Place, a juke joint two hours from Jackson, Mississippi to play with the bluesman Willie King.

Heat is filling my head to bursting. There's a stone on my chest that I can't relieve. Wheels are my consolation. "Who are you?" the spirits ask, and Charley Patton is laughing at me, perched atop a weathervane, wondering why I thought I was so special.

Out of Jackson on Highway 20 we turn onto Highway 56 past Meridien, then a Rubik's cube of small roads through farmlands of soybeans and cotton, thumbnail towns, further and further from the highway. Every time I think we can't make another turn, we continue onto more desolate trails, past tumbledown barns, two-room shacks, a dog marooned on a lopsided porch, peeling paint on rotting eaves, a middle-aged man under a baseball cap on a rusted red tractor, illuminated swaths of green from shortstraw and longleaf pine. Now it's dirt roads, with no human in sight. The radio's on, mostly rock 'n' roll and Christian shows. The signal fades in and out, a preacher howling prophecies like a caged animal, exhalations that spew out of the speakers in waves of incantatory rhythm. TK says "We gonna make those ladies *grind* tonight, brother!" He stretches out the word "grind," so it sounds like *guhriiiiiiiiiiiind*.

When we finally stop driving, it's as if we've arrived at someone's house at the end of a 40-mile driveway. Except the house is a bare-bones shack set on concrete blocks with the words "Bettie's Place" scrawled across the front entrance.

The joint is about sixty feet long and twenty-five feet wide and every inch is beat up. The roof dips and weaves with shingles missing and clapboards rotting at the edge. The screen door won't close properly. To the side of the door, tacked to the facade, are decades old signs for Budweiser and RC Cola, faded colorless by the sun. The inside walls are simply particle board, unpainted, not a piece of sheet rock in sight. There's a small corner for the band under a low ceiling, a modest size dance floor with a tiny bar at the end, and a small room for a pool table.

TK and I haul his bass amp and my guitar amp into the joint and sit outside in two folding chairs waiting for the rest of the band. The drummer drives in, a big bruiser who looks mean but talks to us kindly. A teenager walks in behind him, the drummer's son, who will be joining us on guitar. Willie King pulls up in a white pickup truck.

Willie is in his sixties, stout and strong, with a chiseled jaw and a goatee. His face is inscrutable, he may love you or hate you, no way to tell. He wears a collared shirt, jeans, and dress shoes, topped by a Cleveland Indians baseball cap. He sets up his amp quickly, nonchalant, barely speaking, appraising me with a nod and a near bone-shattering handshake, his big paws calloused from farm work, encircling my unblemished hands. As dusk settles in, people begin to show up, and here more than anything, is what makes me feel as if I were time-traveling back fifty years.

Half the people arrive not by car, but by simply appearing through the fields. They show up from all sides, not just walking down the dirt road that we'd come in on, but by literally traveling down crop rows from nearby farms. This was how music was experienced for thousands of years before the dawn of the car, train, plane. Music was made for a small community, by people in that community, it was social glue of a neighborhood. What do you do on Saturday night? Head to Bettie's Place. I suddenly feel nostalgic for a world that ended long before I was born.

TK has a big grin on his face, "Come *on*, Joel, we gonna make it roll in here tonight. Find us some 'shine to drink too!" Willie sits on a folding chair next to me, unsmiling, counts off a tune, a mean, scarred, beautiful voice, and he strums the simple chords on a beat-up white Stratocaster with his thumb. I settle in, trying my best to speak his language. He's an old-school bluesman, doing classic repertoire from the '40s and '50s, but also his own tunes. Willie has an idiosyncratic way of playing rhythm, hitting bass notes with his thumb and picking some of the notes with his fingers, a style that's his own and yet clearly developed *not* listening to Clapton or Buddy Guy, rather the old-timers like John Lee Hooker, Son House, and Robert Johnson.

He nods to me when he wants me to solo and I dig back into that old sound, the guitar licks that are at the root of my generation's idols, Hubert Sumlin, Hendrix, and Duane Allman. I try not to wear out my welcome, making damn sure not to throw in any jazz licks. After one solo Willie turns his head to me while still playing and says, "Can you turn that damn thing down?" I do.

The dance floor begins to fill, and sure enough the ladies *are* grinding, the place is so small the dancers are almost on top of the band, swinging butts and funky footwork right up next to my guitar strings. I do one wild lick that causes a couple of people to look up from the dance floor and scream their delight, and one lady yells, "White boy can *play*," while another says, "Guitar man makin' my *titties* hard!"

Willie calls the classic "Spoonful," and he puts a delicious twist on it, an extra beat in the turnaround phrase, the kind of anomaly that used to happen all the time, until modern life straightened all the kinks.

We break and I go to the bar, where they serve just PBR and Bud, at $1.50 a pop. Men and women chat outside on lawn chairs, or on the hood of a car, the back of a pickup. A couple of old men sit on the front steps, dressed in pressed white shirts and black slacks, one of them wearing a white fedora with a feather in it. The dialect is so thick I can hardly understand the words, slow and molasses-like. Everyone knows each other, they talk about the weather, gossip about a neighbor. The older guys sit in silence most of the time, expressionless, holding a beer, maybe nodding to someone who ambles by. Folks are friendly, they ask me where I'm from, and how I came to learn the blues, glad that I've come to their favorite spot. The greenery of the trees encircles the yard, a spotted mutt ambles by and then trots back into the woods, the sun eases behind the trees.

That permanent ache in my heart, the stone on my chest, has lifted, levitated off my body by the gritty, funky music.

TK says, "Time to make the ladies *guhriiiiiiind* again," and we rock some more tunes, one chord boogies, 12-bar shuffles, one R&B groove in the style of Curtis Mayfield. Willie has the dancers in the palms of his gargantuan hands, as couples shake all kinds of booty on the gouged wood floor. He never smiles, hardly introduces the tunes, bows his head under the baseball cap, his band listens close, follows his lead.

We end around ten o'clock, and Willie takes my hand one more time after he sets down his guitar, stares at me for a moment. His eyes are deep-set brown, blood shot, wrinkles around them as he takes my measure. There's no way to know what he's thinking, he's staring inside me and through me. Willie finally says, "You're welcome in my band anytime." He then hustles off after he gets whatever small sum Bettie has for him. Doesn't say anything else to the band or the audience, just climbs into his car and hauls off.

I talk with the drummer and his wife for a few minutes, "What's it like up there in New York," he asks, "I want to get up there soon." I tell him it's so full of musicians it's easy to forget you exist, that every kind of music invented by the hand of man is going on there, and he should visit.

One of the older gents still on the stoop gives me a kindly nod as I walk by. He's in dress black pants and a buttoned up white shirt, looks like he's been sitting in the same place for a thousand years. I wonder if anything can phase him, whether if the four horsemen of the Apocalypse rode straight towards him, he'd budge. An affirmation from a man like that is something you carry back home with you, can't hang it on the wall, or sell yourself with it—it's medicine, a healing potion for an ailment you never knew you had.

People are dispersing quickly, starting engines and raising dust, walking back across the fields, laughing, waving goodbye to each other. Crickets sing, a gentle breeze tickles my skin. You can smell the moist, rich earth—it's nighttime at the border of Alabama and Mississippi in a town that has no name, on a spring night where human goodness is overflowing.

We follow a dust trail back towards the known world, through the farmlands and darkened porches. I feel the breath of the ancestors on my neck and arms, and they're singing to me, telling me they're glad that I came their way.

Jim Hall

Scrapple From the Apple

Jim Hall Live! (Horizon1975)

Jim Hall looms over every note of jazz I play, alongside Wes Montgomery. Jim celebrated the unknown. He did so with incredible affinity with his collaborators—his improvising always sounds like it was *meant to be*. There's no excess, no fluff. This courage as an improviser is not a given. Jim lived by it. His music was by turns gorgeous, funny, bold, quizzical, and spare. He was a master of the jazz vocabulary, and he could also free improvise with the best of them.

Jim was one of our great rhythm guitarists. I love how he cited Richie Havens as an inspiration for his rhythm playing. Havens was a completely different player from Hall, a folk musician with a killer right hand on acoustic. No matter—Jim liked his groove, and in fact now and then on a tune like St. Thomas he would launch into some pretty strenuous strumming of his own on his Gibson ES-175 archtop.

Jim's subtle sense of humor shows up in this story. One time a fan asked him how many tunes he knew. Jim considered the question for a moment and said, "Oh I guess about a thousand." He turned to go, and before he got too far, he stopped and turned back around. "Actually," he said, "More like a hundred." This time he made it all the way through the door before he popped his head back in and said, "Actually… just one."

I took a lesson with him in the late '90s, and going over to his West Village apartment was one of the great experiences of my life. Jim and his wife greeted me as if I were an old friend. As I was ushered into his small office, I felt more like a dinner guest than student. Of course he spoke to me about technique, the use of dyads, voice leading, stuff that was foundational to his approach. But the heart of the experience was the music we made. We played a jazz standard and I felt infinite possibility and completely supported—seen, if you will. The way Jim accompanied me was simple yet profound. No matter where I took my playing, he was right there with me, not ahead, not behind—*there*.

This testimony is borne out by everyone I have spoken to who played with him, including Bill Frisell, Julian Lage, and Pat Metheny.

One word for this is empathy. It's a quality that every improviser must have. Some have more than others, and Jim had a ton. His improvisations

Jim Hall at Keystone Korner, San Francisco (1980)
Photo by Brian McMillen.

were ever unpredictable, and yet he was so in tune with his band that it seemed all notes led home. No matter what corner he painted himself into during a solo he found a way out. He could have made a five-minute composition out of two notes.

Jim was a master of understatement. He played less than you expected, which somehow always contained more than you expected. Sometimes he'd turn his guitar down during a solo, to the point where he had no amplification at all—as if to make the point that strength comes not from volume but conviction. It was radical. But as Julian Lage pointed out, he could really hit the guitar hard, too. He presented in a very gentlemanly way, but he felt free to knock the instrument around. Later in life he adopted a few effects, and although I'm not sure he truly integrated things like the whammy pedal into his sound, it was fun to hear him expanding into the digital age.

Jim was a composer first, a guitarist second. He had studied composition at the Cleveland Institute of Music. Everything he played had the consideration, the shape and form that a classical composer might prioritize. Because of this, Jim was asked to be part of projects by some great band leaders, Jimmy Guiffre and his trio, Gunther Schuller's *Jazz Abstractions* with Ornette Coleman, and Bob Brookmeyer's *Traditionalism Revisited*. Sonny Rollins hired him, and I believe it's because Sonny, too, improvised with incredible attention to form. Perhaps his most iconic recordings are the duo albums with pianist Bill Evans, *Undercurrents* and *Intermodulation*. These were a first in jazz. No guitarist had done a series of duos with a piano player in which roles were so easily swapped, in which their approach was so free and yet so rooted in the foundation of the tunes.

His band's performance on "Scrapple From the Apple" from the 1975 live recording, featuring Don Thompson on bass and Terry Clarke on drums, is a marvel of motivic development and band dialogue. Jim's accompaniment to the bass solo is a study in and of itself. The solo he then takes over multiple choruses is truly a conversation with his collaborators. It's one heck of a journey. Although you continually hear references to Charlie Christian and Charlie Parker, there is nary a bebop cliche to be found. Rather he extrapolates on a few motives in a way that is focused, surprising, and great fun. Jim goes in and out of the

Jim Hall. Photo by Brian Carmelio.

key, he uses jarring dissonance, he plays his own idiosyncratic chord melodies, and finally ends up in a burst of rhythm that is reminiscent of Red Garland. It's full of exploratory rhythmic play.

Mainly what you hear is people taking chances.

Jim was not fussy. He seemed incapable of putting on airs. I don't think he would have been caught dead wearing sunglasses on stage, and he never used any of the cliche jazz tropes in conversation. You'd never hear him say use the word "cats," or say, "Let's hang." I was told by Julian Lage, who Jim took under his wing, that Jim didn't like to talk about the old days. He was always looking ahead. He rejected any idea that an earlier era of his life in jazz held romance. He said the so-called good old days, were full of racism, poor working conditions, and low pay. I'm told that as a young man Jim had a problem with alcohol. He sure became a straight arrow by the time I started listening to him. I believe his wife Jane, a psychotherapist, had a lot to do with that. They were tremendously devoted to one another.

Jim was a mentor figure to about every jazz guitarist I've known—from Mick Goodrick and John Abercrombie, Pat Metheny and Russell Malone, to Steve Cardenas and Bill Frisell, and on to Julian Lage and the future. The list is endless. Mick said to a friend once that "being accompanied by Jim Hall is like being in a cathedral." He carried the entire history of the jazz language inside him, from Freddie Green and Charlie Christian up through the most way-out free improviser you could name. I think a great duo project would have been Derek Bailey and Jim.

In performance, at least in the last thirty years of his life, he almost always included some of the same tunes in his set, "Body and Soul," "All the Things You Are" (in ¾ time), "Skylark." Was this playing it safe? Hell no! I advise this approach to anyone. Know ten tunes (or one?) *really* well, not a thousand kind of well. Every time he performed "Body and Soul" it was totally different. He was immune to repeating himself.

Part of the journey in jazz music inevitably involves the blessing of the elders. One of the greatest compliments I ever received was when Jim said in the lesson I took with him—"You know when people say someone sounds 'interesting,' it usually means nothing—but in your case I really mean it. Your playing is really interesting, it holds my attention, and for me that's a big deal." He said this despite my relatively scant knowledge of jazz language at the time.

But my favorite memory of my brief interactions with this casual sage was when we honored him in 2015 in an early incarnation of the Alternative Guitar Summit. I organized a night of his music at of all places, Rockwood Music Hall, a kind of pop venue in Manhattan. Why Rockwood? Better venues refused my entreaties. On this auspicious night folks such as Chris Potter, Vijay Iyer, Vic Juris, Nels Cline, Steve Cardenas, Ben Monder, Liberty Ellman, Gilad Hekselman, and others played Jim's compositions. Jim was in poor health at the time, suffering from back problems, so he elected not to attend the show. He'd been told the seating at Rockwood was uncomfortable. Had we done the show in a theater, he probably would have showed up. Nonetheless he called me on the phone before the show to thank me, and he asked me to send him a recording. I did so, and received a handwritten thank you note from him a couple weeks later as well as a request for the addresses of all the performers so he could write to them too.

What can you say about this small courtesy? That the man behind it was brimming with humanity and consideration for others.

Hubert Sumlin

Goin' Down Slow

Rocking Chair (Chess Records 1962)

by Elliott Sharp

Elliott Sharp is an original thinker and player. He plays guitars that he designs, he makes music based on an obscure branch of mathematics called Fractal Theory, and makes sounds that hardly seem possible. He is also steeped in the blues. I approached Elliott about this book thinking he might write about a way-out improviser from the far fringe. Instead he chose the foundational bluesman Hubert Sumlin, with whom Elliott had a unique, close relationship. Rather than focusing on a single track, Elliott writes about the experience of awakening upon discovering Sumlin's sound.

Rocking Chair! A holy grail album that I'd often dreamed of finding. There it was in the bargain bin at Sam Goody's for 99 cents, now in my hands, found on one of my skip-school-and-hitchhike-into-the-city days. Like so many other suburban white kids, I came to the blues through Paul Butterfield, the Yardbirds, the Stones. But once I heard the sources, the real thing, I was hooked and had to hear it all. Robert Johnson, Blind Lemon Jefferson, Charley Patton, Son House, Skip James—all moved me deeply, but the electric sounds really hit hard. Muddy Waters, Otis Rush, Sonny Boy Williamson, Elmore James, Freddie King ... and Howlin' Wolf!

Wolf's music grabbed me. That feral gravelly voice and the perfect foil, an anonymous guitarist playing acerbic lines, fiery but sweet, guttural but sophisticated, impossibly fast but always lyrical. On first hearing "Goin' Down Slow," I was floored by the strange vocal quality of the two guitar leads, the aggressive angularity and brilliance of the lines. Great as Mike Bloomfield's playing was, my ears told me that he was drawing deeply from a second, unnamed master. There were no credits on the album, and it took me until 1970 to find out this guitarist was Hubert Sumlin.

"Shake For Me," "Killing Floor," "300 Pounds Of Joy," "Wang Dang Doodle" are all prime examples of Hubert's genius. He gave each song a clear identity through a few terse licks filled with emotion, wit, and a Cubist take on melody. Hubert's playing with Wolf proved to be enormously influential and his sonic DNA may be easily teased out of the playing of Jimi Hendrix, Eric Clapton, Jeff Beck, Keith Richards, Robbie Robertson, and so many more.

I first met Hubert Sumlin in a Chicago dive in 1983 where he was alternating sets with guitar trickster Lefty Dizz. The regulars were not pleased that the pool table was pushed to the side so the bands could play.

Hubert Sumlin, Ann Arbor Blues Festival, Ann Arbor, Michigan (1970)

Hubert was playing a yellow Telecaster with humor and relaxed abandon. We spoke a bit about guitars, but I didn't want to bug him on his break. I was just happy to hear him play, and even more so, completely thrilled to exchange a few words with this man whose sound had moved me for so many years.

Through vocalist Queen Esther, my blues band Terraplane was booked to back up Hubert at NYC's Knitting Factory in 1994. I was nervous—could I have ever imagined standing on stage trading licks with one of my all-time heroes? In the dressing room, Hubert was all smiles, calling us "my guys." We played some blues classics and a couple of Hubert's songs. The gig was a gas for all and led to my producing some sessions for Hubert with bassist Fuzz Jones and drummer S.P. Leary at a small Manhattan studio, the legendary Seltzer Sound. There would also be some live recordings.

Before a solo gig of his in a West Village club in 1996, the beginning of a two-night stint, we had a casual and wide-ranging interview. The shows were recorded and after the second night there was an encounter with the club's owner, so typical of the music business. The plan was to record both nights using the house DAT deck with the deal being that I would take the DAT tapes and give the club's owner 1:1 digital copies for his archives. With digital copying, these are absolutely identical. The first night went exceedingly well with Hubert in a great mood and playing some beautifully sweet and insanely wild guitar and singing both his songs and some of the old favorites. I took the tape and ran off the 1:1 copy in my studio before returning to the club for the next evening's show. That night after Hubert's set, I brought the copy of Day 1 and asked the owner for the new DAT to copy. He answered, "No! This one is for me." Rather than get into a discussion with this pig-headed guy, I just called over Hubert's manager, Red, and explained the situation. Soon, Red and the owner were shouting at each other while Hubert and I stood back exchanging little grins and eye-rolls. Red finished the argument with the immortal words: "I'm Jewish, too, so God will punish you if you fuck with me." End of fight and I'm handed the tape.

In 1996, Hubert began guesting on Terraplane recordings and we brought him to Europe a number of times for tours in England, France, and Italy. He always radiated an enormous amount of love to both his audience and to us, his loyal acolytes. I was proud to set up and tune his guitar for him and to back him on those timeless songs. Hubert was always at his best with strong vocalists and with Eric Mingus and Tracie Morris fronting the band, he was stunning. When Terraplane went into our most radical operations, Hubert would find the groove and either dig in to slash unnameable chords or float above with stinging lines.

My last time seeing Hubert was September 2011. He entered producer Joe Mardin's studio for an overdub session for the new Terraplane album *Sky Road Songs* carrying his oxygen tank like a guitar case, chuckling slyly and muttering, "like an astronaut." I hadn't seen Hubert in two years and was surprised by his frailty but reassured by his strong hug and joyful demeanor. Soon we're all laughing over a story about Hubert's early days with James Cotton. He downs an espresso and fingers my white Strat while we play the basic track "This House Is For Sale" on which he'll overdub. Magic in that right hand (not to mention the left)! I've spent many an hour watching like a hawk trying to figure out just how that magic is conjured; a relaxed brushing of the strings with those lo-o-ng digits—totally off-the-cuff cool, but the sounds that emerge are anything but. Hubert switches to my Les Paul for more magic. No matter what kind of guitar he's using (and I've seen him play them all), it always sounds like Hubert!

The 1996 interview:

Elliott: You've put out a number of records in recent years—what's your favorite?

Hubert: I tell you what, it seems to me that *Heart & Soul* with Little Mike on Blind Pig, it ain't stopped yet, I still get a little money. The last one was *Healin' Feelin'*.

Elliott: Do you like recording in general?

Hubert: I do, I really do now. I start to play, hey I found me a style. By listening and looking I said hey, so, "This is me."

Elliott: Did your style of playing with your fingers and not using a pick start to develop when you worked with Wolf in 1953?

Hubert: I think that's what happened, with him and Muddy. When I first started he didn't like what I was doing. I knew it wasn't right cause it didn't sound like I was playing with him. So he fired me, kept on firing me … and hiring me. He called me on a date, a date of need, he called me, said "Let's try it tonight."

Elliott: What kind of guitars were you playing?

Hubert: We had Kays, we had Silvertones, me and Jody Williams. I don't know how many guitars Wolf had. They were Wolf's guitars.

Elliott: When you came back to the band, did your style change the way the band sounded? Would you come up with parts, shape the songs? Your guitar parts define the songs in so many ways.

Hubert: I came up with the parts, the songs. I got together with the horn blowers, baritone and tenor, and we made *300 Pounds*. When those horns came in, it was the greatest feeling. It's finally happening, he's doing his *own* thing. So I put the music to this thing, arrangements in the studio right there before—there was no time—we had a few rehearsals but the horns were always no show. So it was no problem in the studio, I just told them what parts have to be played … bup bup bup … heh heh. I didn't get credit for it. At least seeing my name somewhere, that makes me feel good.

Elliott: It seems like your playing has really influenced all the great players in the world, a fount of inspiration. How does that feel to you, do you reflect on that?

Hubert: You know I'm glad to hear that, I'm glad to know that if I touch anybody, even touched one, you get feelings of a million, you'd be surprised how they come. If you ever heard of hypnotizing, I know, you have this music, sometimes puts you in a state of hypnosis. Well, this is what it will do you. Sometime you hear things, hear things coming through and you know it seems that everybody's hearing them. When I'm reaching an audience, I feel it, I feel it before I'm knowing it.

I feel things that you don't want anyone to know at any particular time. I think about this, I think about that, not about notes, but I'm going to make it sound right. From now on, I promise me, I want to feel the best, do the best. It's not that I feel I haven't paid my dues, I believe you don't get through paying these things, not until you die. Just like you can't get out of this business, you may get out one year, two years or five years but you coming back, brother, somewhere down the line, like starting to walking, it's something that helps. Then you going to find that your playing is going places, it starts to help. I feel proud, you feel like you can do anything you want sometimes. It's a high mountain to climb, this business, sometimes too high but we got to get over it. I believe I can go anywhere in the world and communicate.

I've seen a gang of worlds since I've been born—we survive—I sit back sometimes and think of Lightning Hopkins and Son House, Bukka White, all these guys—the kind of music they were playing, you still hear it today, it may be scattered, you may not hear it in everybody's home, but it's there, it should have gone to the moon. It's management—they could have pushed it.

Elliott: When you were young did other guitarists show you things?

Hubert: On the Delta wasn't too many people that was interested in showing you too much, 'cause they were trying to work themselves. At that time you had to be good, if you just listened. I tell you I was playing wrong all the time! (laughs) But I tell you I can't be too bad, you know what I'm talking about. I got with Cotton [James] when I had my first guitar, the one my mama bought. Cotton went and got this guitar. I saw pictures of Cotton with the clamp on the guitar. I clamped that guitar! My first clamp was a pencil with string wrapped around. I went with Cotton. Cotton said, "I'll use you!" Me, Pat Hare, Cotton, piano player, drummer. Then I left Cotton, went with Wolf cause Wolf paid more money. Sometimes we'd make 50 cents, sometimes we'd make a dollar for a Saturday night.

Elliott: Your sound is so unique, so completely your own. What would you say to young guitarists just starting out?

Hubert: Define yourself, find yourself! Just like you'd get an answer from a dictionary. Find out what you want to do! I knew at eight years old what I wanted to do, I figured I'd be the best guitar player. I wanted to be the best at everything I did.

Lenny Breau with Chet Atkins
Polka Dots and Moonbeams
Standard Brands (One Way Records 1994)

I first heard Lenny Breau's name from Danny Gatton. This would have been the late 70s, in some conversation where I was asking Danny about his influences. Danny was in awe of him. I never saw Lenny's name on a marquee. He died in 1984 before I got a chance to see him perform. I came to learn that Breau was a touchstone for many great guitarists.

Breau played fingerstyle, sometimes with a thumb pick, often nylon string. He had a singular ability to play bass, chords, and melodies at the same time in arrangements that were both technically adroit and gorgeous. He was also the rare player who used a seven string. He once said, "I approach the guitar like a piano. I've reached a point where I transcend the instrument. A lot of the stuff I play on the seven-string guitar is supposed to be technically impossible, but I spent over twenty years figuring it out. I'm thinking melody, but I'm also thinking of a background. I play the accompaniment on the low strings."

Originally from Canada, he based himself in Nashville, and a lot of his repertoire comes from the Chet Atkins school. There's country and Texas swing in his sound, all of it colored by sophisticated jazz harmony. In his use of the nylon string, and the Bill Evans influence, Lenny was similar to Ralph Towner. While Towner developed his own approach to the instrument, largely based on his composing, Breau stayed mostly within the jazz standards tradition. The roots of this acoustic finger style playing goes all the way back to Snoozer Quinn and Lesley Riddle. Merle Travis was perhaps its greatest exponent, but he never moved into jazz harmony. Chet Atkins, with his sophisticated chord/melody blend of country, classical, and jazz, was its grand master—until Lenny came along.

Breau started playing at age eight, and by his early teens was the lead guitarist for Lone Pine Junior, his family's band. The group toured a lot, so Lenny didn't have a typical childhood. While other kids were attending school every day or going to summer camp he was travelling and performing. One day his father slapped him in the face because he added jazz licks to a solo. The kid quit the band. Breau was a fanatic about practicing, and all his playing at an early age eventually turned him into a virtuoso. Tommy Emmanuel, probably our greatest living acoustic guitarist, says in the 2011 documentary *The Life and Legend of Lenny Breau*, "He was already better than all of us by the time he was twelve."

The 1999 documentary *The Genius of Lenny Breau* contains long stretches of interviews with Lenny's friends and associates, mostly in Nashville, and mostly big box or nylon stringers. I had never heard of a single one of them. As someone who considers himself knowledgeable in such matters I was reminded of the many hidden pockets of regional talent, names that don't always make the headlines. Great players, great scenes, and families of like-minded musicians gather in small cells all over the world. Only a few of them come into the greater public 's awareness.

One of Lenny's important contributions was his use of false harmonics. These are bell-like tones rendered by touching notes 12 frets up from a fretted note with the first and second fingers of the right hand, while the thumb and third finger lightly pluck them. It's extremely challenging to execute. Only a few of his acolytes developed the ability to convincingly do this, amongst them are Vic Juris and Russell Malone.

Lenny didn't make a lot of music in the studio, he may have done his best work live. On "Polka Dots and Moonbeams" both he and Chet Atkins play with empathy, dovetailing phrases, each taking a turn playing bass with the thumb, and at the end both add a flourish of false harmonics. The approach is gentle, straightforward, and profuse in harmonic beauty.

They're as technically proficient as any classical maestro of the time.

For contrast, listen to the bootleg of Lenny sitting in with Danny Gatton's Redneck Jazz Band, featuring Buddy Emmons on pedal steel, live from the Cellar Door in Washington D.C. in 1979. There are a few versions available on YouTube, and it's wild as hell. What's interesting is how similar Danny and Lenny sound. I never would have predicted that. On the surface they would seem to be very different. But now I realize how much Danny took from Lenny. Danny was an expert fingerpicker, he would do lengthy interludes that in retrospect emulate the Merle-Travis-meets-Bill-Evans sound that Lenny cultivated. They both loved country and jazz and the many hidden connections between them. Listening to Lenny I even hear some licks that I would hear Danny use a few years later.

Again, the sad story repeats. Virtuosity and the reverence of peers brought neither happiness nor stability. Lenny's drug and alcohol addictions took an early and constant toll. Already leading a somewhat impoverished life as a freelance jazz musician, the need for heroin guaranteed that he'd be broke. He had a disastrous marriage. His wife may have wanted him to remain high, because that way he would never leave her. There were rumors that she was manipulative and even physically violent with him, and some believe she was involved in his death in 1984. He was found at the bottom of a swimming pool, strangled, but the murder was never solved.

Here's a question you often hear about Lenny, and others with uncommon ability— "Why wasn't he better known?" Some existential questions have no answer. Obviously, drug and alcohol problems ruin careers. Less obvious—to play big stages, to make a decent performance income, it's not enough to be a virtuoso. You can play the hell out of the guitar, and essentially only other guitarists will give a shit. Playing with a famous performer helps. Some choose lucrative TV work to supplement their income. Chet Atkins was an arranger and producer. Lenny did none of that.

Pat Metheny taught us many things. Amongst them was that a successful career means not just playing great guitar, but writing music that redefines the landscape. Pat composes in a way that touches more people than if he had stuck to playing standards his whole life. Bill Frisell,

Pat Martino, Kurt Rosenwinkel, too. Lenny came along at a time where few jazz guitarists wrote their own music. There's changing the guitar, and then there's changing *music*. Ideally the former would be enough. Unfortunately, that's not often the case.

But let me argue against myself. Oscar Peterson, a Canadian like Breau, and a virtuoso, rarely composed and had a tremendous career from an early age. The fact is, that given the choice between listening to Lenny or Oscar Peterson, the average person would likely choose Oscar. For one, Oscar's music is buoyant, incredibly exciting, and deeply based in the swing tradition. Lenny's music was far more intimate, introspective. That doesn't mean it was any less beautiful. The truth is the guitar has certain limitations compared to the piano when it comes to playing jazz. The piano was built for and by jazz. The range that Oscar could achieve with 88 keys dwarfs what's possible on acoustic guitar.

The next generation of masters, Scofield, Frisell, Stern, Metheny found ways to broaden what was possible on the electric guitar—electronic effects, the advances made by luthiers, new influences outside jazz as well as new instrumental combinations. Somehow this makes the music of Lenny Breau even more precious, though. Extraordinary craft with the simplest of materials.

Kurt Rosenwinkel

Ezra

Caipi (Heartcore 2017)

By 1980, Pat Metheny, John Scofield, Bill Frisell, and Mike Stern began to dominate the jazz guitar landscape. Their era seemed to stretch on forever, the oxygen theirs. Call them the "Big Four." By the late '90s the only additional person to attain their visibility and influence was Kurt Rosenwinkel.

His 1998 release, *The Next Step*, changed the jazz guitar world. Suddenly everyone sounded like Kurt, they bought hats like his, emulated his rig, his tone, and even his body language. Listen to Kurt's improvising and it's obvious why. Fully saturated in bebop language, he created a modern, signature sound grounded in stunning compositions.

But here's something none of the "Big Four" did—write and *sing* a song to one of their offspring.

Kurt's run at the jazz club Smalls in the late 1990s, in which his band developed his most iconic pieces, is the stuff of legend. It culminated in the seminal record *The Next Step*. Since I lived on the west coast in the '90s I never saw them. I saw Kurt play in a trio when I visited New York City, heard him with Paul Motian, but never with his storied band. By the time I moved to New York he had moved to Germany.

I got to know Kurt when he became one of the core teachers in my guitar camp. Sitting next to him on stage and playing a tune was an education. It's one thing to see a master play, and another to actually play *with* him or her. Kurt's mastery of the jazz language was beyond anything I had ever experienced, or maybe even imagined. Although this might seem obvious listening to his records, it smacks you in the face when you're playing a standard two feet from his tuning pegs. Growing up, Kurt didn't have the typical detours into rock, punk, funk or whatever. He was obsessed with jazz. By age 18 he'd already played Monk's "Reflections" more times than I might in two lifetimes.

But then there's "Ezra," which Kurt wrote and sings. When I heard this piece it gave me an even greater appreciation for the man's music and for him as a human being. The song makes me a bit teary-eyed. The fact that somebody with this much intellectual savvy, this much technique, can leave it all behind to make music this simple and vulnerable is something deeply touching. Kurt doesn't have a trained voice. It's sort of like listening to Charlie Haden sing. It's all heart. He could easily have brought in a great vocalist, but I'm glad he didn't.

The composition itself is fairly straightforward, though a couple of surprising harmonic moves add color and impact. It's the lyrics that I admire most. I have no children. This song makes me wish that I could write a song to a son I don't have. My relationship with my father was extremely distant. In a million years he would never have said, much less sung, anything to me this unguarded. There are a lot of mistakes Kurt could have made in this song. It could easily have been maudlin. He could have overdone it, made it more complex than it needed to be. Instead, it feels timeless, and how many pieces of music can you say that about?

I hear some corollary between "Ezra" and Wayne Shorter's work on *Native Dancer* with Milton Nascimento—folk-based material, jazz improvisers, and lyrics and melody both tuneful and memorable. This was a period where Kurt was exploring Brazilian music, collaborating with some of the best young Brazilian musicians, resulting in the album *Caipi*.

Jazz can be quite the macho affair. There's a lot of emphasis placed on chops, and a history of cutting, a show can become a gladiatorial battle. Although this mindset is changing, for some it's still about speed, being hip, being dominant. It's a relief, then, to hear a song like "Ezra," to which any sentient being might relate.

Of course, there's a long history of vocals in jazz, but mostly based on standards. There are vocals all over my work, Frisell's work with Petra Haden, Metheny's wordless vocals in his group with Lyle Mays, Tuck Andress with Patti Cathcart. But "Ezra" is something different. It's more kin to Dylan's "Forever Young" than Hoagey Carmichael. Kurt steps up as his own singer, composes his own lyrics. It's not a song about romantic love, someone's foolish heart, Georgia, the moon, or Valentine's Day. Neither is it abstract, boppish, or caked with dreaded scat singing. It's a man expressing love to his son. That's what I call deep.

Kurt Rosenwinkel with Jeff 'Tain' Watts Trio, BIM Amsterdam (2018)

Elliot Ingber

Alice in Blunderland

The Spotlight Kid (Reprise 1972)

by Henry Kaiser

There were several occasions when writing this book when I was stumped on some fact or another. Invariably when I called Henry Kaiser he would have the answer. Henry knows more about guitar arcana than anyone I know. I knew if I asked him to write a guest essay he would choose a guitarist and track I would never dream of choosing, which was the point. I had never heard of Elliott Ingber, and only occasionally listened to Captain Beefheart. But clearly both are powerful, if wayward voices. This was a rich and far out time for electric guitar. Here is a guitarist who was steeped in the African American blues of the time and yet found his own freaky path.

Back in October 1971, I went to see Captain Beefheart and the Magic Band at the Sargent Gymnasium at Tuft's University in Medford, Massachusetts. This gig was shortly prior to the early 1972 release of their album, *The Spotlight Kid*. I was 19 years old, and I had seen earlier incarnations of the Magic Band going back to 1967. I had all the Beefheart albums in my record collection, and I knew all the songs. Something was different at this show; there were new songs and unprecedented improvised blues-rock guitar solos on many of the tunes from a guy with long hair and a bushy beard who reminded me of a 1940's image of King Neptune. This was Elliot Ingber, stage-renamed by Beefheart as Winged Eel Fingerling.

Stepping out of that time frame into now, I can tell you a bit about Elliot.

He was born in 1941 and lived in the Minneapolis area in his youth. Early on he was a master of American electric blues, years before the idiom caught on in England. In 1959 he was on the very first recording of surf music: the single "Moon Dawg" by his band The Gamblers. The flip side of that single, "LSD-25" is also the first mention of the psychedelic drug in American popular music. Elliot was in Zappa's Mothers of Invention for their first album, *Freak Out!* He was also associated with early Little Feat and the Fraternity of Man. He spent a few years in different incarnations of Beefheart's Magic Band.

Back in 1971, I was sitting on the floor of the gym, super-enjoying the show, when they suddenly played a 7-minute instrumental with a long

Magic Band. L-R: Elliot Ingber, Don Van Vliet, Denny Walley, Bruce Fowler, John French (1975)

solo from Elliot. This was "Alice in Blunderland," a tune that had been played on previous tours with solos from Beefheart on sax, as well as shorter solos from Elliott and Zoot Horn Rollo (aka Bill Harkleroad). But at this show it was given over to one long, very psychedelic solo from Mr. Ingber. The floor fell away from underneath me during his solo. I was transported to music spaces and dimensions that I had never visited before. I was a fan of Bay Area psychedelic bands, Indian music, blues, African music, post-WW-II classical composers, Zappa, etc. But nothing had ever taken me to the place that Elliot's improvisation suddenly moved me to. I was not a musician; I had never played any instrument. But at one moment during the solo I suddenly knew that I had to go buy a guitar the next day. Which I did—purchasing a black Fender Telecaster at nearby Tavian Music. Oddly enough, I can listen to the live audience recordings of the show on YouTube today and identify the exact moment when I realized my guitar destiny.

I had my own cassette recording that I had made at the show. I listened to it hundreds of times during my first years of playing. "Alice in Blunderland" was the first tune that I learned to play on guitar. In 1972 *The Spotlight Kid* was released with a studio version of "Alice" on it. Elliot's solo on the album was the first solo that I learned from a record, lifting the turntable needle up and down to learn it phrase by phrase and slowing it down to 16 RPM to figure out the fast flurries of notes. Over the years, I have played the song dozens of times live with more than twenty different bands.

Now, 53 years later in 2024, I have a discography of more that 450 albums that I have played on. I've recorded in many idioms—free improv, jazz, blues, rock, Hindustani music, Korean music, contemporary classical, Malagasy music, country music, and more. In all those genres I catch myself channeling things that I learned from Elliot's "Alice in Blunderland" solo. It's not licks, or harmonic ideas or melodies, though— it is narrative modes and storytelling, plus connection to some external spirit world, plus heart and soul. Everything I do on guitar connects back to that moment in the Tufts Gym in 1971 being transported by Elliot.

Elliot was in and out of the Magic Band several times. During one of the late-70s incarnations I was introduced to him and we remain friends. Now in his eighties, he could be classified as a recluse. But whenever

Pity the Genius: A Journey through American Guitar Music in 33 Tracks

Henry Kaiser & Eliott Ingber

we speak on the phone, he picks up the conversation exactly where we left it a year or two before. Elliot knows things about guitars and music that few others know. He has his own highly unique, and unfortunately not-so-well-documented, approach to blues guitar. In that department I'd put him on a cosmic level of soul and originality with Peter Green and Mike Bloomfield.

It's a strange thing to have your most significant guitar hero be somebody that most folks have never heard play guitar; as well as never have heard of. I have so many musical heroes who I idolized before I ever touched a guitar, and I've had the good fortune to play and record with many: Derek Bailey, Jerry Garcia, Sonny Sharrock, Cecil Taylor, Richard Thompson, David Lindley, Terry Riley, Freddie Roulette, John French, Wadada Leo Smith, Ray Russell, Harvey Mandel, Amos Garrett, John Abercrombie, Fred Frith, Bob Weir, Sylvestre Randafison, Barry Melton, Zakir Hussain, the list goes on and on. But for me, Elliot Ingber and "Alice in Blunderland" was where guitar *playing* began for me. Some spark jumped from Elliot to me back in 1971, and things have never been the same since.

Vic Juris

Time Remembered

Songbook (Steeplechase 2000)

Sunday evening at the 55 Bar, Vic's monthly West Village residency. Jay Anderson on upright, Anthony Pinciotti on drums, Vic's out front with a semi-hollow body hanging from a leather strap. He's in a suit jacket, slacks, dress shoes, his graying hair neatly combed back as he leans into the neck of the guitar and lets loose a string of thick, eerie chords on a slow, quiet tune. The sound is lush inside the funky dive with its worn, wooden walls, its whoosh of history, so wonderfully and completely New York. Vic is expressionless—a handsome man, some wrinkles, but fit at age 65. Then a slight grimace as he starts to burn on the Miles Davis tune "E.S.P.," a fast, oblique progression that has always eluded me. He somehow makes sense of it, surprising, practiced, elegant, and sure.

The crowd, maybe 22 of us, is hushed. The bartender tries to stir a drink without making a sound. Things heat up, there's an exchange of phrases, a buoyant, swinging pulse. It occurs to me that I, and others, take Vic for granted. In any other town he'd dominate, be feted. But it's *the city*. He's been playing like this for decades, bars this size, known but not known, part of the pulse of the town.

Vic, who died of liver disease in 2019, was amongst a handful of go-to players for jazz bandleaders in New York from the late '70s on.

Pity the Genius: A Journey through American Guitar Music in 33 Tracks

You want your music done right? Call Vic. He knew what to play—big bands, singers, duets, anything really. When Vic joined saxophonist Dave Liebman's band in the 1990s, one of the first things Dave noticed was how serious Vic was. He would record the rehearsals on cassette, and several days after the session would call Dave to ask about a few things he wasn't sure he understood. Dave was asking him to play music that was more technically advanced than what Vic had been doing. He had to navigate the A to Z harmony that's Liebman's trademark, pretty Brazilian tunes, bitonal slash chords, free playing, long Coltrane-inspired modal jams. He did it all without breaking a sweat. He was relentless in his desire to give Dave what he needed. They played together for 23 years.

I met Vic in the early 2000s. He'd played with any number of jazz greats, Phil Woods, Rufus Reed, Richie Cole, but I was unfamiliar with his work. I asked him to participate in the Alternative Guitar Summit's first concert series in 2011 with a duet partner of choice. I expected him to name someone whose playing was like his. He chose Mary Halverson. I loved that—a totally different player than he, and at that time still somewhat unknown. Their dialogue was effortless, idiosyncratic, and just plain fun. He also played in our 2015 tribute to Jim Hall. There he was straight ahead, a master of the bebop language.

It was a revelation when I listened to his first record, *Roadsong* made in 1978. He played everything at blinding tempos, clearly influenced, perhaps too influenced, by Pat Martino. Had he been doing speed before the session? It was as if a different artist were on the record. I'm told that in those times he was a drinker. Back when they met Liebman described him as a "New Jersey guitarist." I asked what he meant by that. "Rough around the edges," was Liebman's reply. Vic's playing changed over time. He got sober, slowed down a little, and learned a ton about harmony from Liebman. He was always extremely honest with himself.

What strikes me most about his nylon string solo rendition of the Bill Evans composition "Time Remembered" from 2000 is the *certainty* you feel. It was the same thing I felt seeing him live. His command of the instrument is never in question, he never falters. His approach is pianistic, containing a spectacular chord vocabulary. It's a beautiful, lonesome, harmonically dense tune and Vic gives it plenty of soul—but there's an edge, too, some dissonance and bite. The New Jersey guy is still there.

Vic wasn't afraid to step on the fuzz box and rock out. Sheryl Bailey was in a group with him that played Hendrix tunes, and she described the delightful torment of always hearing him push her to the limit. When you get someone at Bailey's level saying that, take notice. Vic was also a beloved teacher at various NYC-based schools for much of his life, his students are everywhere. In the 2000s Vic began to focus more on his own material, often in a trio format. These records are good. But I find his real milieu to be the jazz repertoire, especially more advanced tunes that few people play, such as Scott Lafaro's "Gloria's Step," Wayne Shorter's "Delores," and the aforementioned "E.S.P."

Once I went to see Vic with a guitar pal. During the break Vic warmly congratulated my friend for placing high on the recent *DownBeat* magazine guitar poll. Then he smiled and added, "Hey what about me, why am I not in there? What am I, chopped liver?" We all laughed.

The next day I decided to look at the poll. Vic was somewhere near the bottom. I had placed above him. I was horrified. I learned that Vic had

Vic Juris. Photo by Scott Freidlander.

never placed high on this list. It was another lesson in how meretricious the whole business is. If you know anything about jazz guitar, you know Vic Juris was a far more accomplished jazz player than I was or ever will be. That's not to diminish my efforts in music at large. But *DownBeat* is a *jazz* magazine. And Vic was one of the best jazz guitarists alive for decades. In one of those twisted, sick ironies, he ended up finally placing high on the list the year he died. It was shameful.

Vic would have had a good laugh about this. He was a gentleman, a sweet, generous soul. He didn't take these matters too seriously. But it hurt him inside. He knew his value, and being overlooked is hard to ignore. Here's what we have to remember. To his peers he was held in highest regard. The real poll is who's working. And on any day of the week Vic would be on the bandstand with great musicians, getting paid to do so, and doing a great job every time.

I saw Vic perform only a few weeks before he died. He sounded as good as ever. I had plans to record with him—I'd written a tune called "Sunday Night with Vic," inspired by seeing him at his residency at the 55 Bar. But he died before we had a chance to go to the studio. There's never enough time.

Derek Trucks

Gravity

I Am the Moon III: The Fall (Fantasy 2022)

In Indian music there's a concept called *gharana*. It refers to a school of performance practice connected to a family dynasty of musicians. It indicates lineage, style, and approach and may stretch back centuries. For instance, the famed sarodist Ali Akbar Khan hailed from the Maihar gharana; its cornerstone was his father Allaudin Khan who profoundly influenced many of the 20th century's greatest performers including Ravi Shankar and Nikhil Banerjee. If you're born into a gharana you're brought up with exposure to its traditions, it surrounds you. Simply by being in one of these families you're celebrated if you take the path of music. You still must practice hard, and live up to the family's expectations, but if you do, certain stages will be automatically opened to you. In India, as elsewhere around the world, birth confers certain privileges.

   I wonder if you could say that Derek Trucks is from a gharana? A relatively new one, The Allman Brothers gharana, the blues/ rock/ Southern soul gharana. He was, in fact, born into a royal family, the nephew of Allman's drummer, Butch Trucks. I assume he was exposed to incredible music from a very young age. It's downright spooky the way he built on the roots his uncle Butch Trucks laid down. In his autobiography Gregg says that when he first heard Derek he felt like he was hearing his brother reincarnated.

Some kids of famous musicians who decide to go into music seem to be pulled in opposite directions. One direction beckons—be yourself it doesn't matter who your parents are. The other whispers—be like your parents, that's who we're really here to see. You get immediate recognition and interest, and you also get compared and reviled. The industry is heavy with bitter children of celebrities. Some progeny of superstars have a terrible time accepting that doors are often opened for the wrong reasons.

Luckily Derek seems to not have suffered from any such maladies. From his early teens he was on a tear, and he hasn't slowed down, his music keeps getting richer and richer. As a slide guitarist he exists in a class all his own. It seems to me that whatever his Uncle Butch and his parents said or did was pretty perfect.

Derek studied the music of Ali Akbar Khan and has worked some of the phrasing and tonality of northern Indian music into his blues phrasing. He's also a huge jazz fan, and apparently cranks John Coltrane on the tour bus. It's a broad palette.

It's one thing to play a series of lovely phrases. It's another to play perfectly in tune with incredible tone. But Derek does much more. He has a particular superpower, his ability to attain a level of drama in the climax of a song. When you play slide, or bottleneck, you are mostly playing with one finger, like a sitarist. Derek and others fret notes here and there to augment the slide, but it's not possible to play a lot of notes, you can't rely on speed. You can't really do arpeggios either. Derek builds with melody, articulation, movement into upper registers, a keening, voice-like wail through two Fender Super Reverbs on ten. If you listen to his latest work, for instance the Song "Gravity," you hear nuance in each note. Check out the way in which he moves towards or away from the pitch, the speed and width of the vibrato, the ornaments surrounding the pitch, the weight of the right hand when he hits the note, the octave work, the timing, the tuning, the intensity built on repetition and perfect synchronicity with the rhythm section. It's like he's a great aria singer.

I first saw the lad when he was sixteen. He played a show at a Jewish

Community Center on West 67th St., on the same block I was living at the time. The day before, I'd met him briefly and heard him sit in with Warren Haynes and the boys at a Gov't Mule show at the Beacon Theater. He would soon join Warren in the Allman Brothers Band, helping them kickstart a late-career surge that continued until 2014. As a teenager he was already good. I remember thinking how amazing he'd be in a few years and, to my delight but not surprise, it happened. The guy just keeps getting better and better.

Derek Trucks and Warren Haynes

Dennis Budimir

The Blues, Sprung Free

Sprung Free! (Revelation 1968)

with Bill Frisell

During the COVID-19 pandemic I hosted several teaching summits online. One of my favorites included Bill Frisell and others talking about 10 guitar tracks that had shaped them. Frisell's choices taught me a lot about his own music. Most of his selections emphasized group interplay, artists that were lesser known, nothing heroic or overtly sensational. One included a name unknown to me, Dennis Budimir. I was thrilled to learn about someone new.

In October 2023 Bill came over to my house and we continued our discussion. Dennis was on the cutting edge of the post-bop jazz scene in L.A. and New York City in the late 1950's. He made several recordings, most notably as a sideman to drummer Chico Hamilton in a band that featured Eric Dolphy. In fact, Budimir lived with Dolphy not far from where I currently reside in Brooklyn. He made his own bracing trio records in the '60s with a young Gary Peacock on bass and Bud Shank on sax. Dennis replaced Jim Hall in Hamilton's band, which suggests his aesthetic. The two had plenty in common.

By the late 1960s Dennis was in a *totally* different environment. He wound up back in his hometown of L.A. as part of the famed studio outfit The Wrecking Crew. Budimir subsequently played on hundreds of important recordings—Joni Mitchell's *Court and Spark*, Bobbie Gentry's *The Delta Sweetie*, Frank Zappa's *Lumpy Gravy*, Ravi Shankar's *Improvisations*. He was *the* studio player of this era, and he earned the unstinting respect from his peers. One of his fellow studio aces, Tim May said in a Vintage Guitar interview with Jim Carlton, "Dennis' contribution as a guitar player is unsung in that he was always the anonymous studio pro who played great, in tune, in time, and always correct. He had the musicianship to be a major force in the demanding Los Angeles studio guitarists' scene, which didn't always come with a lot of high-profile accolades." Meanwhile, his days as a touring jazz player ended.

Here is what Bill says about Dennis: "My first teacher, Dale Bruning, in Denver, told me everything. I had discovered Wes Montgomery and he started telling me about all the folks like Jim Hall, Jimmy Raney, Johnny Smith, and then Dennis Budimir. This is maybe 1970. I listened to a recording by Dennis, and it felt like that was the future—the next step after Jim Hall.

When you hear "Miss Movement," [from the 1959 Chico Hamilton record] it's really crazy. His lines go a little farther than you're expecting. Something about his choices, the phrasing and melodies almost go off the rails—no cliches, and really surprising. So I got all excited about him—but then I was disappointed when I found out he'd become a studio musician. I got this gig with Carla Bley, Michael Mantler, Steve Swallow, and Nick Mason (Pink Floyd's keyboardist). I'd recently met Swallow, we're hanging out—I asked if he'd heard of Dennis Budimir, I thought I was being hip or something. Steve had definitely heard of him, you know Steve had lived on the west coast. So I was saying 'He's totally sold out. And now he's just one of those studio guys, it's such a drag, 'cause he was destined to be the next guy, the future of jazz guitar. And then he just went commercial.'

Swallow got mad. I got scolded. He said, 'You have no idea what was going on. How can you say that? You don't know what was happening in this guy's life, or anything about this situation. You can't possibly judge him.'

So I learned something. It was a big lesson. I mean, I'd never say that today.

It turned out Dennis had come to New York in the late '50s, and he was doing well, living with Eric Dolphy, and then he had to go into the Army. So then he comes back and moves back home to LA, but a lot of his friends are gone. So, where's the work for a jazz guitarist? He doesn't know exactly what to do. Someone says, 'Hey man, I got this recording with Frank Sinatra, why don't you come?' So he's on this record date playing all the crazy New York jazz stuff and gets reprimanded. But then he realized, oh, I have to play the right thing. And the next day

Chico Hamilton Quintet : Wyatt Ruther–bass, Nathan Gershman–cello, Chico Hamilton–drums, Eric Dolphy–reeds, Dennis Budimir–guitar (1959)

he got a call again. And then he just fell into that studio work. He's on everything we ever heard, but we never even knew that he was there."

Bill and I listened to the long solo Dennis takes on his 1968 track "*The Blues—Sprung Free!*" Bill's reaction connected the dots for me about how Dennis transcends guitar tradition: "So he's already going out of the key, and the solo just started. Really different. That's wild. I love how much time he spends in the low register. In a blindfold test you might think Dennis is Miles Okazaki. It's that exact tone with the Charlie Christian pickup. He's pushing off the edge of what they knew. It's still connected to the tradition and everything, but—it's way out. There are also some records with Dennis playing with Billy Bean. They're just sitting around in the kitchen or something. Dale told me about Bean. People say he was the closest thing to Charlie Parker on the guitar. "He's outrageous, Billy Bean." When Bill and I were done talking, we listened to "The Blues—Sprung Free!" one more time. Clearly Dennis had a vision at a very young age of where the instrument could go. The whole track is delightfully eccentric, and still based firmly in jazz traditions.

Later, I found an interview with Dennis by radio host Jake Feinberg. They spin those same records Bill and I listened to, and Dennis, who hadn't heard them in decades, says, "Man, that guy plays his ass off!" He seems truly pleased to revisit his former self. Dennis recalls that at the age of 17 he was already turning heads. As I listened to the interview I wondered, how was it that these two entities co-existed inside Dennis? The cutting-edge youngster and the esteemed studio elder?

I asked Bill about meeting and jamming with Dennis in 2021.

"Well, it's a long story—Wilco (the rock band) came to Seattle, and I sat in, and they just handed me this guitar. It was a Nash Telecaster, and Bill Nash was there. Then about three weeks later I go home and there's a box, and he had sent me a guitar! I ended up going down to his shop and he showed me all around. I had just recorded the record *When You Wish Upon a Star* that uses movie themes. Nash told me his dad, Bill Nash, had been a studio trombonist who'd played on everything from 1945 on, and he told me about Bob Bain, another storied studio guy. I told him how much I liked Dennis' records.

So he set up a lunch in L.A. where all these guys from the old studio days showed up, including Budimir and Bob Bain. Dennis was thrilled

I knew his work, and I got him to sign a record. He was really gracious and kind. And then this guy from *Fretboard Journal* set up this other meeting with Bob and Dennis where we played and talked. It was just so cool to meet those guys."

Bill and I talked some more about what it was that set Dennis apart in those early records—he was one of the more transgressive players of his time, slippery phrasing, more like a horn player than some of their contemporaries. He didn't have that boxed in feeling that some guitarists have. A true improviser.

Why is that important?

I'd like to try to explain in a way that might be understandable even to a non-musician. To Bill, and to most jazz musicians, the goal is not what we already know—it's discovery. New frontiers. We're looking for something that's never happened before. Let's say we listen to back-to-back solos. The first is beautifully executed, but derivative. It's been done. The second has new ideas, it makes you raise your eyebrows in surprise, laugh. It may even be a little sloppier as the player stretches. Bill would likely prefer the second. You can hear that in Dennis' jazz playing. It's the more remarkable because of how young he is, only 21 at the time of the Chico Hamilton recording.

Picture two plates of pasta. One tastes exactly like you'd expect. It's good, no complaints, you'll walk away full. But the other makes you exclaim, "My God I've never tasted anything quite like that. It was different—spicy!" And then you remember that meal for a long time. That's Dennis Budimir.

There were a number of great players in the late '50s, some of whom I've mentioned in this book. Most of them found that the life of a jazz musician was untenable. Johnny Smith left the touring life to work in a music store and play a local gig in Colorado once a week. Tal Farlow mostly retired in the late '50s and worked as a sign painter. Jimmy Raney's career was cut short by alcoholism and disease. Billy Bean also suffered from alcohol abuse. The Los Angeles studio scene kept many players going— Barney Kessel, John Pisano, Herb Ellis, Jimmy Wyble, and Dennis.

It's tantalizing to think where Budimir would have gone if he had stayed in New York and lived the jazz life. Instead, he became a vessel for other peoples' dreams. Dennis described this abrupt transition in the *Vintage Guitar* interview: "I had to quickly reassess my values. And the more I got into the studio thing, I realized that while some areas of rock and roll and country may not be as sophisticated as jazz, in order to be very good at those forms it requires knowledge, talent, skill and conception similar to what you need in any music, including jazz and classical… My view has broadened so I analyze it from that point of view and the musicality within that framework."

My talk with Bill ended with us agreeing that the people behind the scenes in the studio, like Dennis, had earned our undying respect. It was as honorable and enviable a living as the jazz touring life.

And so this piece ended… until I stumbled upon information I didn't anticipate.

I happened to mention my essay on Dennis Budimir to a guitarist who knew him well from the mid-1980s and on in Los Angeles. He shared with me, somewhat reluctantly, that becoming a studio ace embittered Dennis, that in general he felt he was playing music by hacks. Little of it was artistically satisfying. The scene was populated by people who preferred talking about their mansions and cars to music. He became cynical and dark—and rich. In learning to copy all styles, which is the calling card of a studio player, he lost his own. The high life changed him, made him condescending. Dennis refused to go out and play his own music, he disdained "low money" gigs in clubs, derided any younger player who chose that path. Better to become a lawyer than a player of any kind.

It's impossible to hide from life, isn't it? Romance comes and goes. At the end of every day, every year, every moment, we end up with ourselves and the choices we've made.

Curtis Mayfield

People Get Ready

People Get Ready (ABC Paramount 1965)

Curtis Mayfield was the sound of mid-1960s Black empowerment. That time was Curtis and Curtis was that time— protests on college campuses and city streets demanding equality and justice, race riots in Detroit, Watts, and D.C. This was socially conscious music filled with aspiration that spoke to frustration, intimidation, segregation, dignity. The young people were more than ready. Curtis was a musical Muhammed Ali. "No," he said, "We're not staying silent anymore. We're speaking the truth." Ali had his fists, Curtis had his honey-toned falsetto.

One of the remarkable things about "People Get Ready," or another of his huge hits "Keep On Pushin,'" is that they instantly became universal. The concerns of the ghetto, articulated in Curtis' simple poetry, spoke to every socially aware sentient being on earth. Let's take *another* moment to consider the monumental gift of Black music to America. It leads us.

I remember when my hometown, Washington D.C., was set on fire after Dr. King was killed. I stood up on a hill near where we lived by the National Cathedral and saw the orange flames and black smoke bellow up from the inner city below. I stared and stared. I felt something burning in my chest. I knew almost nothing, but even then, age eleven, I was moved, stunned, scared. It made me part of what I am today. I

Pity the Genius: A Journey through American Guitar Music in 33 Tracks

knew I had to live a life that was part of the solution not the problem. Later that week my mother shoved us in the car. She said she wanted us to see these neighborhoods, see the truth of what had happened. Row houses were still smoldering on U street. Buildings all over Northeast D.C. were scorched, glass, plaster, household items littered the ground. It was a war zone. Some buildings were boarded up and the words *"Soul Brother"* were scrawled across the plywood. "Mom, what's a soul brother," I asked? She explained as best she could.

Curtis was the quintessential soul brother.

This music was central to the Civil Rights movement. With songs promoting change and self-affirmation, fans started referring to him as "The Preacher." But he disdained that title. He wasn't looking to be an oracle, just a musician who spoke truth to power.

How often does one artist sum up the concerns of an entire body of people, connecting them, making them feel like *family*? The more fragmented our world, the harder it is to imagine. And yet here we are sixty years later claiming to be more unified because of Facebook.

The songs of the mid- and late-1960s live on—the era of Black music that gave us "Respect," "Dancing in the Streets," "Midnight Hour," and "My Girl." These songs are still played across the world. They've lasted for a reason. All the technology in the world, the synthesizers and the deejays, cannot recreate the vibration that brilliant folks like Curtis birthed. Marvin Gaye, Stevie Wonder, Prince, and so many more all began where Curtis left off.

When Curtis was writing, the guitar was king. Most every band centered the guitar, it drove the pulse, gave the tracks the raw propulsion and sting that a piano could never do. You can't extricate Curtis' lyrics from the guitar. His words, melodies, and guitar parts are one.

Curtis' guitar parts appear to be fairly simple. They have an everyman quality to them. But they're not easy to execute. You need to study hard to get the feel and articulation right, there's nuance. The art of rhythm guitar is mostly lost now. It's fallen out of fashion in much contemporary music. Some of the younger players who do play funk often play in a way that feels lifeless. They play with a ruthless perfection. It's a like an electric fireplace instead of a crackling hearth. I want to name check one young man who is getting it right—Chicago's own Isaiah Sharkey.

Where does the real rhythm and blues sound come from? The Black church. Look to Pops Staples, the scion of the Staple Singers, a seminal group, contemporaries of Curtis. The Staple Singers, just like Curtis' band, The Impressions, which was the soul group Curtis was in from the late '50s until 1970, started with Jesus and eventually branched out into the concerns of the street. The echo of gospel piano playing is in Curtis' guitar work.

Mayfield and the Staple Singers were both from Chicago, a righteous town with its own sound and feel, the place where modern gospel began. I know Chicago players who claim they can tell right away when a bass player is from Chicago. I think it has to do with the fact that so many players in the city, including blues greats like Howlin' Wolf, migrated from the South, the Mississippi Delta, and New Orleans. Southern sweat-drenched stank with all that urban energy and vitality.

It's interesting to note that Curtis tuned to an open F# chord, and he used his thumb, not a pick. That's part of what gave him his sound. When he started writing for his own band, notably on the iconic 1972 album *Super Fly*, the parts got a little more complicated. I learned that there was another guitar player involved in this band, Craig McMullen, who complemented Curtis. He played the parts that needed a pick.

Curtis Mayfield (1972)

McMullen is an example of a fabulous studio rhythm player who did his job virtually unseen.

Some of the most delicious, lovingly crafted, and soul stirring guitar playing of my lifetime has been in the realm of rhythm and blues. As a child I was smitten by the early Motown hits, and later in life by the Stax catalog. This is vast terrain. A number of mostly invisible African American rhythm guitarists were behind these tracks—Larry Veeder, Robert White, "Wah Wah" Watson, Joe Messina from The Funk Brothers in Detroit, Henry Fawcett from Johnny Taylor's band, Bobby Eli from Philly. Better known were Steve Cropper from Stax, Cornel Dupree who was with Aretha and so many others, and James Brown's mainstays Jimmy Nolen and Catfish Collins. We owe a debt to these players that can never be paid. Curtis Mayfield was on the leading edge of it all, starting back in the late 1950s. He affected everyone. Hendrix adopted plenty of his rhythmic phrasing, the pull-offs with the pinkie, the sliding 4ths, the two and three note hammer-ons.

"People Get Ready" has a few of Curtis' signature touches. First, the staccato stabs on offbeats, followed by the lovely interlude that uses sliding 4ths, a hammer-on, and then a chiming, arpeggiated chord. Curtis boiled everything down to its essence. Bare bones parts like the keel of a boat. The anthemic lyrics couldn't be more direct. Most songwriters spend their whole lives searching for lines this pure and pointed, this essential.

Mayfield was one of the first African Americans to control his own publishing, to start his own label, to have control over all his creative and business affairs. It got harder once he fell out of fashion, and there were tough times. He withstood it all. In 1990 he was paralyzed from the neck down when a lighting rig fell on him during an outdoor show. Curtis kept performing, even recorded another record, delivering his vocal line by line from a wheelchair, as he summoned his breath. He lived another seven years.

Called the "Gentle Genius," Curtis blazed a trail that connected soul music with its political potential. He lived in epochal times and made poetry about what he experienced, with both his voice and guitar. His imprint is everywhere from Bob Dylan to Seal, Lauryn Hill, Beyonce, and John Mayer. His music and legacy of social activism will last far into the future.

Afterword

I began the book with these words:

I've found there are only three antidotes to the insanity of the world we live in—the love of another human being, the untamed wilds of nature, and art. In this book I honor a few of those who with a guitar managed to bring some shape, beauty, and love into our lives.

What of this shape, beauty, and love?

Of all the arts, music is the most mysterious. I love it most for this reason. Part of its mystery stems from the fact that music is invisible, untouchable. It short circuits our stubborn minds, and our limited reasoning. We may be able to explain a sentence of Shakespeare's. But we cannot explain why a melody makes us cry. It's often been stated that one can't unravel music with words. Maybe true, maybe not, but that was never my goal. My goal was to offer the music, and with it a snapshot into the inner workings of one of the most intimate acts a human being can perform—sharing the deepest part of themselves with sound.

Knowing the story behind these tracks, to whatever degree that story has been made available to me, has offered me insight into the human condition, lessons in vulnerability, courage, devotion, and fragility. And to me these matters are sacred. What actually happens to these bold souls when they perform their magic? We know what their music does for us. What does it do for them, or to them?

While writing this book I found myself caring in a quite personal way about these heroes of mine and the lives they led. I felt invisible connections, in many cases with people I never met. Where an artist succeeded a small part of me rejoiced, and where they fell short, or suffered, some small part of me suffered too. When Arthur Rhames was lying in the hospital bed speaking to Vernon Reid with such innocent optimism about where he hoped to take his music days before his death, part of me was in the room. When Sister Rosetta was giving one of her triumphant concerts at the height of her career, a part of me was in the audience. I revisited the bar stools, the smells, the extraordinary eruptions of noise from the audience during a Danny Gatton show. I picked up my guitar more than once to play along with Pat Martino and Gil Goldstein, seeing if I could ingest the deep silence and explosive attacks in Pat's phrasing. And I also imagined what it might be like to record Pat's track only months before suffering an aneurysm that robbed him of every memory he'd ever had.

There's the music, and there's the body and soul behind the music.

In another culture and time some or all of these artists would be considered holy people, those entrusted to be a medium between invisible gods and all too visible human beings—priests, if you will, of our culture, without any of the religious baggage. This doesn't confer upon them absolution for their faults. However, it demands our respect. If nothing else, I want to believe these musicians earned our attention.

And for those, like Jimi Hendrix, who *were* made into deities? Let's remember not just the mountaintop they reached but the long slog up the steep road they took to get there. Let's remember Jimi for the trauma he felt that led to the making of "Machine Gun," not just the ecstasy of its creation.

If you add all 33 of these tracks together, what do you have? An extraordinary range of human experience, a vast ecology of sounds that inspire, mystify, delight, tear apart. We see the range of the guitar, how it wails, moans, screams, whispers, struts, and swings. No other instrument tells the story of life in America like the guitar, save perhaps the human voice.

I often despair when I read the latest headlines, attempting to ingest the daily quotient of suffering, the latest war, the poverty and hunger, the petty and arrogant political battles, the struggle for equity, the overwhelming need that floods every corner of our world. In those moments I turn to these artists, and many more like them, and of course to my own art. In that I feel blessed. When I hear Allan Holdsworth's soaring, keening tone on "Sphere of Innocence," Blind Willie's Johnson's bark and wail as he slides up to the octave, Joni Mitchell's ode to transience accompanied by Larry Carlton's ghostly, ephemeral fills, I regain balance. Some redemption for our collective lunacy is suggested. Some reason and justification, beyond explanation or knowing, of why we're here on earth.

All around us we see so-called solutions for the terrible problems we've created for ourselves. Thank goodness there is art that offers no solution. It simply exists, not as a means to an end, a remedy or a pat explanation. Music is a window into the human heart, whose depths are unknowable, whose abundance will always lead us.

About the Authors

Guitarist, composer, arranger, lyricist, writer, educator, and vocalist Joel Harrison has "created a new blueprint for jazz" (*New Orleans Times-Picayune*). A Guggenheim Fellow (2010) he has released 25 CDs as a leader on seven different labels since 1994. Harrison's music may be founded on jazz but veers into classical, rock, country, and all manner of American roots music.

Succinctly described by the *New York Times* as "protean... brilliant," he has also written multiple works for chamber ensembles and is an active film composer, having worked on the Oscar-nominated *Traffic Stop* and the Sundance awardee *Southern Comfort*.

Harrison is the author of *Guitar Talk: Conversations with Visionary Players* as well as *Modern Jazz Standards for Guitar*. He has contributed articles to *Premier Guitar*, *DownBeat*, *Jazz Times*, and other music periodicals, and is also a writer of fiction.

Harrison studied guitar and jazz with Jimmy Wyble, Mick Goodrick, and Charlie Banacos, and composition with Joan Tower and W.A. Mathieu. He attended the Ali Akbar Khan School of Music and was a member of the Agbekor W. African Drum and Dance troupe in the 1980s in Boston.

Harrison is the founder and director of the Alternative Guitar Summit, an annual festival devoted to new and unusual guitar music. Pat Metheny has called the Summit "one of the most interesting and distinguished forums for guitar on the planet."

In 2017 Harrison founded the Alternative Guitar Summit Camp, a meeting place for some of the world's best improvisers and generally considered the foremost guitar teaching camp in the world (alternativeguitarsummitcamp.com). He runs the educational site Guitar Unlimited (patreon.com/guitarunlimited) and teaches master classes in the U.S. and Europe.

Joel can be found online: joelharrison.com
Facebook: facebook.com/joelharrisongtr
YouTube: @joelharrisongtr
Instagram: instagram.com/alternativeguitar

Guest Contributors

Nels Cline is a guitarist and composer of uncommon versatility and imagination. Crisscrossing the worlds of free improv, jazz, rock, and much more he has released over 30 CDS as a leader. Cline has been lead guitarist for the band Wilco since 2004.
nelscline.com

Adam Levy is a guitarist and educator who has supported some of the most respected singers of our time including Norah Jones and Lizz Wright. He records and performs his own music and has been hailed as one of the most lyrical players of our time.
adamlevy.com

Vernon Reid is a founder of the Black Rock Coalition and is a co-founder of the seminal rock bad Living Colour. Criss-crossing funk, rock, punk, jazz, and free, he has worked with some of the greatest artists of our era including Jack Bruce, Bill Frisell, Mick Jagger, Public Enemy, and Bernie Worrell.

Henry Kaiser has been a champion for experimental guitar music for close to five decades. His catalog of more than three hundred releases tell the story of a player with infinite curiosity and endless appetite for the sonic road untraveled.

Bill Frisell is a defining guitarist of our era. Straddling all manner of American music he has been lauded far and wide for his poet's touch and boundless vision.
billfrisell.com

Elliott Sharp has been a central figure in the avant garde and experimental music in scene in New York City for close to forty years. He has released eighty -five recordings ranging from orchestral music to blues, jazz, noise, no wave, and techno music.
elliottsharp.com

Photo Credits

Artist	Page	Credit
Uncle John	2	Personal collection – Joel Harrison
Arthur Rhames	8	KamandiTheLastBoyOnEarth, Public domain, via Wikimedia Commons
Pat Martino	15	Philippe Agnifili, CC BY-ND 2.0
Danny Gatton	18	Nizzman, CC BY-SA 4.0, via Wikimedia Commons
Danny Gatton	22	Photo by Nancy Keener
Roscoe Holcomb	26	Bess Lomax Hawes collection (AFC 2014/008), American Folklife Center, Library of Congress
Emily Remler	30	MCJazz / Marty Ashby
Allan Holdsworth	41	Gm7b52001, CC BY-SA 2.5, via Wikimedia Commons
Blind Willie Johnson	44	Columbia Records "race series," Public domain, via Wikimedia Commons
Jimi Hendrix	51	A. Vente, CC BY-SA 3.0 NL, via Wikimedia Commons
Jimmy Wyble	54	Public domain
Roy Buchanan	61	Carl Lender, CC BY-SA 3.0, via Wikimedia Commons
Sister Rosetta Tharpe	68	James J. Kriegsmann, Public domain, via Wikimedia Commons
David Lindley	73	Rob Bruce, CC BY 2.0, via Wikimedia Commons
"Thumbs" Carllile	77	Public domain
Prince	80	penner, CC BY-SA 3.0, via Wikimedia Commons
Jerry Garcia	89	Carl Lender, CC BY 2.0, via Wikimedia Commons
John Abercrombie	94	Tom Marcello CC BY-SA 2.0

Pity the Genius: A Journey through American Guitar Music in 33 Tracks

Artist	Page	Credit
John Abercrombie	95	John Abercrombie © Roberto Masotti / ECM Records
Sonic Youth	101	Photograph by Monica Dee. Distributed by SST Records., Public domain, via Wikimedia Commons
Ritchie Blackmore	105	Gladstone~dewiki, CC BY-SA 4.0, via Wikimedia Commons
Ralph Towner	108	Brian McMillen / brianmcmillenphotography.com, CC BY-SA 4.0, via Wikimedia Commons
Ralph Towner	110	© Scott Friedlander
Cornell Dupree	112	Public domain
Cornell Dupree	114	Lionel decoster, CC BY-SA 3.0, via Wikimedia Commons
Joni Mitchell and Larry Carlton	116	Kenneth C. Zirkel, CC BY-SA 4.0, via Wikimedia Commons
Joni Mitchell and Larry Carlton	116	Capannelle, CC BY 2.0, via Wikimedia Commons
Jim Hall	126	Brianmcmillen, CC BY-SA 4.0, via Wikimedia Commons
Jim Hall	128	Photo by Brian Camelio
Hubert Sumlin	132	Eatonland, CC BY-SA 4.0, via Wikimedia Commons. Photo by Jeff Titon.
Kurt Rosenwinkel	143	Dirk Neven, CC BY 2.0, via Wikimedia Commons
Elliot Ingber	147	Private collection
Elliot Ingber	148	DiscReet Records promotional photo
Vic Juris	151	© Scott Friedlander
Derek Trucks	155	autumnwaldenpond, CC BY-SA 2.0, via Wikimedia Commons
Dennis Budimir	159	Public domain
Curtis Mayfield	165	AVRO, CC BY-SA 3.0 NL, via Beeld en Geluid Wiki, an initiative by the Netherlands Institute for Sound and Vision.
Joel Harrison	171	© Scott Friedlander

Also from Cymbal Press

cymbalpress.com

Life in E Flat – The Autobiography of Phil Woods
Book of the Year - Jazz Journalists Association
Life in E Flat – The Autobiography of Phil Woods is the life story of the legendary saxophonist, composer, band leader, and National Endowment for the Arts Jazz Master. Look for it in paperback, hardcover, and e-book at cymbalpress.com.

Praise for Life in E Flat
"*Life in E-Flat* is a gift, a compelling and entertaining memoir by one of the leading alto saxophonists in jazz for 60 years. Phil Woods was a star soloist, influential lead alto player, savvy bandleader, underrated composer-arranger, and consummate studio musician. He was also a charismatic storyteller with a typewriter—literate, funny, insightful, self-aware, with a keen eye and ear for details that reveal character, including his own personal failings. Heroes and colleagues like Charlie Parker, Dizzy Gillespie, Quincy Jones, Benny Carter, and Ben Webster are drawn in quick, astute sketches. Observations about the music business, jazz education, and the vagaries of the jazz life are laced with wisdom and sardonic wit. The book is also an invaluable portrait of world that has vanished: Juilliard at midcentury, the band bus, the bustling post-war bebop academy of the streets, the New York studios of the '60s, the European jazz scene of the early '70s, and the energy and excitement of a remarkable life lived among some of the greatest giants in jazz history."
—Mark Stryker, author of *Jazz From Detroit*

"Phil Woods's voice on the page is as raw and lyrical and unmistakable as the sound of his alto. If you want to really know about The Life—the true day-to-day of a working jazz musician, with all its agonies and ecstasies and tedium and the ever-exciting challenge of getting paid something like what you're worth for playing your heart out—look no further. *Life in E Flat* pulls no punches and tells no lies."
—James Kaplan, author of *Sinatra: The Chairman*, *Frank: The Voice* and *Irving Berlin: New York Genius*

Also from Cymbal Press

cymbalpress.com

Jazz Dialogues with Jon Gordon

Backstage, on the bus, or in the studio, saxophonist Jon Gordon, winner of the prestigious Thelonious Monk International Jazz Saxophone competition, chats with several generations of great musicians. From Jay McShann to Renee Rosnes, *Jazz Dialogues* lets the reader hang out with dozens of jazz artists to learn about their careers, influences, and the dues they've paid. These candid, poignant, and often hilarious conversations paint a first-person portrait of jazz history.

Artists include: Jay McShann, Eddie Locke, Cab Calloway, Maria Schneider, Jan Garbarek, Ken Peplowski, Tim Hagans, Mark Turner, Hank Mobley, Bill Easley, Doc Cheatham, Scott Robinson, Eddie Bert, Phil Woods, Danny Bank, Billy Drummond, Ben Monder, Charles McPherson, Milt Hinton, Ben Riley, Bill Stewart, Art Blakey, Jon-Erik Kellso, Eddie Chamblee, Jimmy Lewis, Chuck Redd, Bill Charlap, McCoy Tyner, Melissa Aldana, Ronnie Mathews, Kevin Hays, Jim McNeely, Steve Wilson, Red Holloway, Barney Kessel, Joe Williams, Quincy Davis, Bob Mintzer, Dick Hyman, Lee Konitz, Leroy Jones, Renee Rosnes, David Sanborn, Gil Evans, Don Sickler, Sean Smith, Sarah Vaughn, Derrick Gardner, Sylvia Cuenca, Harold Mabern, Gene Bertoncini, Mike LeDonne, Essiet Okon Essiet, Bill Mays, and Joe Magnarelli.

Praise for Jazz Dialogues
"Jazz Dialogues is a rarity among books about jazz: It's a book about people—the individual creators who devote their lives to the making of this profoundly individualistic art. It took a writer who's a first-call musician himself to capture the way jazz artists think and feel, on the bandstand and off. From Cab Calloway and Doc Cheatham to Maria Schneider and Steve Wilson, Jon Gordon brings us face to face, mind to mind, heart to heart, with dozens of fascinating musicians. Like a great player in a jazz band, Gordon knows not only how to play, but how to listen."
—David Hajdu, author of *Lush Life: A Biography of Billy Strayhorn*

Also from Cymbal Press

cymbalpress.com

Ruminations & Reflections: The Musical Journey of Dave Liebman & Richie Beirach

The Jazz Book of Two Lifetimes

NEA Jazz Master saxophonist Dave Liebman and pianist Richie Beirach have enjoyed a fifty-year friendship on and off the bandstand. They've performed with Miles Davis, Elvin Jones, Stan Getz, Chet Baker, Freddie Hubbard, and their own bands. Ruminations and Reflections takes readers on a rollicking journey through their musical lives. Along the way, they share their views on jazz education, prominent musicians, and musical preparation. Liebman and Beirach pay tribute to their musical mentors, tour their discography, and suggest essential recordings to study. The book's conversational style will engage students, professionals, and music lovers alike.

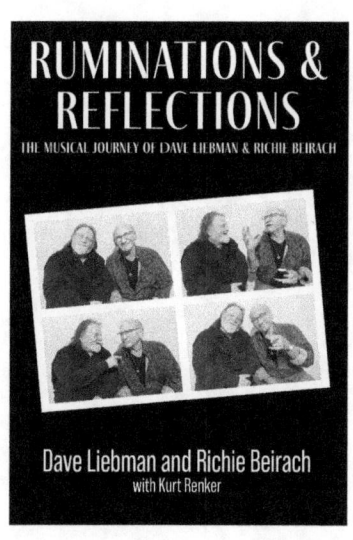

For Fans of Jazz Masters and Legends

Ruminations and Reflections showcases never before told anecdotes and opinions about musical legends including John Coltrane, Bill Evans, McCoy Tyner, Jack DeJohnette, Wayne Shorter, Michael Brecker, Randy Brecker, Chick Corea, Lee Konitz, Sonny Rollins, Herbie Hancock, and Wynton Marsalis. Jazz fans will delight in the in-depth analysis of over twenty of this duo's best recordings, providing insight and history to this important discography.

Praise for Ruminations & Reflections

"We really don't have an exact name for musicians like Dave and Richie. Across decades of recordings and concerts, their aspirations obliterate the definitions of any single genre. This volume reveals the deep insight and wisdom required to resolve their shared quest for meaning in music. Both are master players who continue to strive for what goes beyond and what lies beneath. Reading their words and following their stories in this wonderful book affirms the feeling that they share on the bandstand as one of the great long-term partnerships in this music." – Pat Metheny

www.ingramcontent.com/pod-product-compliance
Lightning Source LLC
LaVergne TN
LVHW020929090426
835512LV00020B/3287